PRAISE FOR MY PORTION FOREVER

"In *My Portion Forever*, Georgia Schmeichel has portrayed thoughtful and sensitive insight into the difficulties, expectations, and responsibilities of a Christian marriage in the midst of the world's demands. While trying to balance raising two young children, teaching in a small reservation school, providing support for her mother's grief in the death of her father, and functioning as a rancher's wife in rural South Dakota, the main character learns what it means to listen to the voice of God. This compelling novel will find the reader thinking often of the memorable characters and their struggles."

— Marilyn Schlekeway

"This first-time novel by Georgia Schmeichel is a winner! With each character and scenario, Georgia develops real-life issues, and she expertly incorporates the Word of God to prove God is our source of strength and our portion forever."

— Karen Rickerl Muellerleile

"Once you start, you will be compelled to read this book to the end to discover how things turn out for the memorable and charming characters of Cedar Creek. *My Portion Forever* is a sweet story that reminds me that only God Himself can meet all of my needs."

— Courtney Stiegelmeier

"Georgia has written a touching story of faith and family. She weaves a tale of the choices we make, the weight we carry, and the hope that transcends it all. Her message will lead you further into the Father's arms where you will find all that you need."

— Sarah Hanks,
Author of *Mercy Will Follow Me*

For my husband Dale,
You've always been the one.

MY PORTION
FOREVER

Copyright © 2021 by Georgia Schmeichel

All rights reserved.

No part of this book may be reproduced in any form or by any electronic or mechanical means, including information storage and retrieval systems, without written permission from the author, except for the use of brief quotations in a book review.

Unless identified differently, scriptures are quoted from The Holy Bible, New Century Version®, copyright ©1987, 1988, 1991 by Thomas Nelson, Inc.

Scriptures marked RSV are from the Revised Standard Version of the Bible, copyright 1952 [2nd edition, 1971] by the Division of Christian Education of the National Council of the Churches of Christ in the United States of America. Used by permission. All rights reserved.

Scriptures marked NRSV are from New Revised Standard Version Bible, copyright © 1989 National Council of the Churches of Christ in the United States of America. Used by permission. All rights reserved worldwide.

Softcover ISBN: 978-1-953314-41-3

Ebook ISBN: 978-1-953314-42-0

Library of Congress Control Number: 2021907889

Published by:

Messenger Books
30 N. Gould Ste. R
Sheridan, WY 82801

My flesh and my heart may fail,
but God is the strength of my heart and my portion forever.
Psalm 73:26, RSV

He is enough;
Always!
Georgia

PROLOGUE

Something was terribly wrong, but the niggling fingers of dawn couldn't pry open the sleepy cocoon that enveloped Tanna. She had a decision to make as soon as she opened her eyes. After tossing and turning all night, the shrill ring of the alarm snapped her eyes open to full awareness of her problem.

The letter.
The wedding.
The choice.

Yesterday started as an ordinary August day. The sky was a clear, brilliant blue, and the air had been washed by a refreshing morning thunder shower. Most of Tanna's pre-wedding doubts were behind her, and then, the local postmaster, a middle-aged man who had known Tanna since she was a toddler, toppled her carefully arranged plans with a simple telephone message.

"Tanna, we've found a letter for you…um… It's postmarked January second…from…uh…let's see, Josh Schmidt at…uh, South Dakota State University in Brookings, SD.

Somehow it got wedged between the counters in the post office. You understand these things rarely happen. We hope it's nothing important..." The voice droned on while Tanna's thoughts flew back to New Year's Eve.

NEW YEAR'S Eve at her parent's home was a tradition. For as long as she could remember, Tanna's parents, Sam and Sarah, had invited their neighbors, the Schmidts, to feast on her dad's secret-recipe chili and her mom's mouth-watering cornbread before ringing in the new year with a midnight sleigh ride. Leftover Christmas cookies and hot cocoa warmed them after the ride.

When Tanna was a child, everyone had piled onto the sleigh pulled by Sam's blue roan draft horse, Storm. As the children grew into adults, a full load was too much for the sleigh, so the parents opted to stay home while Tanna, her brother Matt, and his best friend, Josh Schmidt, braved the cold to carry on the tradition.

This year, Matt would be in Aberdeen where he was celebrating New Year's Eve with his girlfriend. Using the excuse that she didn't want to be the only single there, Tanna turned down an invitation for tacos and a movie with the young adult group in one of the nearby churches. She didn't want to let herself hope Josh would come to the party, but that's exactly what she found herself doing as she declined other invitations.

The day before the party, Tanna overheard her parents talking about their New Year's Eve party while she loaded the dishwasher in the kitchen.

My Portion Forever

"Sam, do you think we should invite some new people to the party this year?"

"Why? It's always been just us and the Schmidts. Still sounds good to me."

"But, Sam, Matt won't be here and Josh may not come. Tanna doesn't want to spend the evening listening to us reminisce about the good old days."

"Sarah, just let Tanna decide what she wants to do." Sam ended the conversation and Tanna whispered another prayer that Josh would be there. Maybe, just maybe, this time he'd see her as something other than a kid sister.

Tanna scavenged her closet the day of the party trying on outfit after outfit, wanting something that would make her look sophisticated and mature. She rejected one after the other, not wanting to be too obvious about her motives. If Josh came, he had a way of looking at her like he knew what she was thinking. She finally decided on a pair of skinny jeans and a sweater that matched her azure eyes.

She continued to pray she would have a chance and the nerve to finally tell Josh how she felt about him. "Please, Lord, let Josh come tonight, and give me the courage to tell him."

Tanna repeated the prayer all day and jumped when the phone rang. She chose not to ask her mom who called after she heard her say, "Okay, thanks for letting us know. We'll see you tonight."

So far, Tanna had kept her feelings for Josh a secret from her mom, but lately she'd noticed "the look" Tanna knew so well. It had appeared every time she or her brother had tried to hide something from their perceptive mom. Without saying a word, Sarah sent a clear message: "You might as well tell me now before I figure it out, and I always do."

Storm was munching on hay in the barn and patiently waiting to be harnessed to the sleigh for his yearly jaunt when the Schmidts arrived in their red Ford pickup truck. The house and yard were still decked for the holidays in Sarah's festive and inviting style. The lights twinkled on the trees, and candles flickered on the window sills, casting an inviting glow inside and outside. Soft music and the faint smell of pine and gingerbread filled the air, making Tanna wish this was the beginning of the season rather than the end.

Sam and Sarah opened the heavy wooden door to greet their neighbors, and Tanna took one final look in the mirror before stepping into the hall where she heard Mr. Schmidt's hearty laughter as he hugged her mom and shook hands with her dad.

"We never see you folks now that our sons don't spend every waking minute turning our hair gray!"

"Hey, no fair picking on me. Without Matt here, I'm outnumbered, and Tanna's no help. She's still a good girl." Josh winked and flashed a playful grin at Tanna.

Caught off guard, Tanna rolled her eyes and hoped her wry smile hid her frustration. Why hadn't he noticed she was no longer a teenager but a college graduate who had been teaching at the local high school for four and a half months? Yes, she lived with her parents, but that was only until she paid off some of her college loans. Josh would rent a dreary room from a stranger before he would live with his parents after college.

He loved his parents and their home, but it wasn't his style to be dependent on his parents if he could afford to live on his own. Joining the National Guard was his strategy for working his way through the state university without owing anybody anything even if it took him extra years to complete his degree. He sought a business degree only because his dad wanted him to have an alternative to farming and ranching.

Supper conversation was dominated by her dad and Mr. Schmidt reminiscing about Josh and Matt's teenage pranks.

"Remember the night the boys taped bright, yellow caution tape across all the cafeteria doors after basketball practice? When the cooks came the next morning, they were afraid to go in because they thought something criminal had happened."

"Every meal served in that cafeteria was a crime when I was in high school." Mr. Schmidt laughed at his own joke. "Didn't you boys have to mop the cafeteria floor for a month after that, Josh?"

"It was only a week, probably because we confessed after everybody made such a big deal about missing breakfast. We didn't get off as easy at home, though. We were grounded for a month."

"Mom made Matt clean up the kitchen every night for a month to teach him how hard the school cooks had to work, but I thought it should have been longer. Didn't you guys always say to me, 'You do the crime…'"

"'…You do the time.'" Josh finished Tanna's sentence. "But when did you ever do anything wrong, Little Miss T?"

"You'll never know." Tanna hoped her enigmatic expression told Josh that he didn't know everything about her.

"I don't remember if I made Josh do anything besides coming home right after basketball practice and staying there until school the next day. Somehow, Josh always charmed his way out of any long-lasting consequences with those pleading, brown eyes of his." Mrs. Schmidt smiled at her son.

"You boys were never mean or destructive, and I remember Matt assuring me that there was no reason to worry. He told me it was a good thing he and Josh were Christians, or they would have gotten into some serious trouble." Sam stopped to think for a moment before shaking his head. "That's what he told me after I found that *Welcome to Cedar Creek* road sign in the trunk of his car. You two always avoided crossing the line we set for you even if you often came close enough to touch it."

Josh rose from the table ready to end the embarrassing table talk. "Who's ready for a sleigh ride?" Reaching for his empty bowl and plate, he looked from person to person at the table.

"Not tonight, Josh. These old bones are headed for that recliner right there." Sam pointed to the chair positioned by the fireplace in the large, open living area adjacent to the dining room and motioned for Sarah and the Schmidts to follow him.

Sarah stopped to clear the bowls and plates from the table, but Josh took them from her. "We got this. Right, Little T?" Josh flashed that lopsided grin of his and winked at Tanna, causing the dreaded heat to travel up her neck to her cheeks.

Dropping her head to hide the blush, she gathered the silverware and napkins willing herself to take control. "You're the boss, Josh. Always have been. The little sister doesn't get a choice, does she?" Tanna hadn't meant to sound so snarky, but Josh just laughed.

"Somebody needs a nap!"

Shooing his mom and Sarah away, he carried the dishes into the kitchen and waited by the sink for Tanna to join him. Dangerously close to tears, Tanna answered most of

Josh's questions with short, simple answers. He finally gave up trying to engage her in conversation until they finished and put the last bowl away.

"Are you still up for a sleigh ride or are you too tired?" Josh searched her face with a concerned look.

Tanna hesitated, knowing the conversation she wanted to have with Josh would either develop into the relationship she longed for, or it would end their easy friendship.

I'll help you, the voice in her heart whispered.

Tanna faced Josh with renewed confidence. "I'll meet you outside after I put on my coat and boots."

JOSH STOPPED Storm at the top of the hill overlooking her parents' ranch, and they silently surveyed the panoramic view before them. The gently sloping, snow-covered hills stretched into the velvety blackness of the night sky dotted by a few twinkling stars and the lights of a ranch miles away. The glowing moon and murmuring breeze seemed to be urging Tanna to say something, but when she shifted in her seat to face Josh, he turned to her with a concerned expression.

"Are you too cold? I better take you home, or your mom will have my hide. I promised I'd get her little girl home safely."

"Why do you always think of me as a little girl? I've grown up, and I'm old enough to have a little girl of my own!" Tears sprang to her eyes as she struggled to control her frustration.

The wounded look in Josh's eyes made her regret her outburst, causing more tears to flow. Gently wiping her tears with his thumbs as he cupped her face in his warm hands, Josh studied her face, and she could see in his deep, brown eyes that he already knew.

"It won't work, T."

The expressive face she had dreamed about so often was now clouded with anguish. Josh rested his hands on her shoulders and looked up at the sky as though searching for something.

"I have nothing to offer you, Tanna. We're as different as two people can be. You've always—and I mean always—walked the straight and narrow, and I've... Well, let's just say, I've taken a few detours. You know exactly where you're headed. You always have. I'm still searching. If I had definite plans for the future, you'd be right there, but don't expect anything from me. I have too many complications in my life right now, and the last thing I want to do is string you along when Mr. Right could be waiting for you around the corner."

Determined to hide her deep disappointment, Tanna swiped at her tears and attempted to lighten the mood. "Don't toss clichés at an English teacher."

She had hoped to bring back the light in his eyes, but instead, he turned away. The lonesome call of a coyote filled the air as they began the cold, silent trip back.

Now, after all these months, the letter he'd written two days after their talk said he'd thought and prayed about it on the long drive back to college.

I can't make any promises right now, but I'd like to see where this takes us.

Tanna didn't know why Josh hadn't tried to contact her

when she didn't respond to his letter, but she had taken his advice and found "Mr. Right."

At least that's what she'd thought until yesterday.

―――

THE NEW SEMESTER after Christmas had brought several new teachers. One was Joshua Swenson, a history teacher, who attended her church and was the exact opposite of Joshua Schmidt with a few exceptions. Their names, of course, were strikingly similar, and they had both served in the National Guard in Iraq. That's where the similarities ended.

The new Josh was quiet and reserved, but Tanna was attracted to him despite the differences - or maybe because of them. Most significantly, he was stable and ready to make a commitment, and her parents welcomed his willingness to help on the ranch. More than once during their courtship, Tanna had asked herself if this Josh was simply a substitute for the other, but in time, she came to see the qualities in Josh Swenson she knew she'd always wanted in a husband. He was dependable, thoughtful, and attentive.

More importantly, he was a devoted follower of Jesus. Still, she sometimes longed for more spontaneity and passion to go with the love she was beginning to feel for him. Her mom counseled her to pray and wait, but then, out of the blue, Josh Swenson proposed in an uncharacteristically romantic manner. Tanna hesitated but then decided he must be the answer to her prayers for a godly husband. Plans were made for a late summer wedding in the same location where Josh had proposed.

Tanna was blissfully preparing for her happily ever after. Until now...

CHAPTER ONE

Ten Years Later

"Jaz, what are you doing? We can't wait any longer, or we'll be late for school!" Tanna stood outside her daughter's room, urging her brown-eyed six-year-old to hurry and hoping Josh would hear her. He was usually lost in his sphere of coffee and online newspapers every morning if he was in the house when they left for school. She wondered how her husband could be so oblivious to the struggle she faced. Making sure their children were ready to leave early enough to reach the school at the time mandated for teachers was quite a feat.

Six-year-old Josephine Anne Zelda, Jaz for short, always wanted to put "just one more thing" in her backpack, and four-year-old Tucker Joshua liked to dawdle over his cereal and pretend he was a cowboy out on the range, eating his grub before the big round-up. The only way Tanna could get her energetic, blue-eyed towhead out to the car quickly was to ask him why his horse was so slow.

Her own appearance had become less important to her lately. Whatever clean and comfortable sweater and pair of slacks she could find became her automatic choice. Choosing jewelry and other embellishments simply took too much effort, and she'd fallen into the routine of pulling her long, blond hair into a ponytail after her shower. It was either that or cut it short enough to wash and wear, but she wasn't quite ready for that yet.

If she wore any makeup at all, it was a few quick brushes of concealer to cover the dark circles under her eyes and a swipe or two of clear lip gloss to moisten her lips. Her unblemished complexion and the natural pink tinge that lit up her cheeks and lips made her look much more put together than she felt.

"Once in a while Josh could lend a hand zipping their coats and buckling them into their car seats," Tanna muttered to herself as she slid behind the steering wheel.

Have you told him you need help?

"I want him to notice!" Her audible response prompted her children to lean forward inquisitively in their seats behind her.

She smiled into the rearview mirror as she put the car in gear. "Mommy is just talking to herself again."

The twenty-five-mile drive to school every morning was both blessing and blight. The barren country roads seldom saw more than one car at a time, and the daily journey gave her a little time to clear her head if her children weren't talking about their own concerns for the day. Most often, she replayed the argument with Josh from the night before. It was almost always about the little time Josh had to spend with his family.

This wasn't what she had expected when her mom had asked if she and Josh wanted to buy the ranch following her dad's sudden death. Matt and his wife had declined the offer, preferring to stay in Denver with their daughter. The opportunity to give her children the same carefree childhood she had experienced thrilled Tanna, but what she hadn't anticipated were the financial obligations that required her to go back to teaching.

Josh put in fourteen-hour days too frequently, and they quickly learned that a teacher's schedule and a rancher's calendar didn't mesh. If he had time off during the winter, she was in the thick of her school year. When she had a break during the summer months, he spent every daylight hour working outside and then fell into bed exhausted after eating supper.

But something else was on her mind this morning. Yesterday afternoon, the dean of students had stopped at Tanna's classroom during her planning period to introduce a new freshman English student who would start school today, more than halfway into the second semester. Tanna had written down the pronunciation of her unusual name so she could remember it. *Shĭ-vawn*, a pretty name, but she wondered how it was spelled. The defiant look the new girl gave Tanna forecast a looming challenge to her authority and patience.

It wasn't unusual for students to transfer with only three months left of the school year, and those students had usually made the rounds of living with different relatives. When a new student started school in Cedar Creek this late in the year, he or she was often behind the other students. Some had missed large chunks of their education by going to a variety of schools in numerous states. Sometimes, their worldly education far exceeded their knowledge of the fundamentals in English, science, and math. The heartbreaking part was that many were bright, talented students who had fallen so far behind that they would never catch up.

Don't be one of the lost ones, Tanna hoped for both of their sakes.

"Mommy, Tucker won't leave my backpack alone. He's messing up my papers and Teacher will blame me."

Tanna's thoughts turned back to her children as she slowed for the approaching town speed zone.

I have to concentrate on what I'm doing. It was a familiar rebuke, one she gave herself every time she drove while her mind was elsewhere.

The wide streets of Cedar Creek on the Rushing Waters Indian Reservation in South Dakota were lined with an eclectic mix of old and new buildings. Some were towering, dilapidated reminders of the thriving community that once existed, while others were new and squat, erected for practicality rather than style.

Sighing as she approached the brick school building that was partly old and partly new, Tanna reduced her speed to avoid students haphazardly crossing the street. The hot breakfast available every morning beckoned even the most reluctant pupils.

Tucker gave Tanna a quick hug goodbye after Tanna unlocked the back door of the school. He was always anxious to see his preschool teacher, and Tanna was grateful she didn't have to coax him anymore. Positive that his dad couldn't possibly get along without him at home, there had been many tearful mornings at the beginning of the year. He liked school and his teacher, but Tanna suspected that the snacks available for anyone who hadn't eaten breakfast played a part in his eagerness to go to his classroom in the morning.

Jaz stopped outside her first-grade room where some of her classmates were talking and laughing. As Tanna climbed the steps in the older part of the building, she moaned when she realized she still had to develop a game plan for dealing with the new student.

"Good morning!"

Monica, the biology teacher from the classroom across the hall, approached Tanna as she juggled her book bag and purse, trying to work the key into the ancient lock on her classroom door.

"Morning." Tanna was too preoccupied with working out strategies for the new girl to show much interest in Monica's latest news. Gossip was always plentiful in their small community, and Monica was the chief purveyor on this floor. Tanna's conscience told her not to listen but her hunger for adult conversation often won.

"What do you think of the new girl?" Monica closed the door as she walked into the room. "I hear she was expelled from her school in Sioux Falls, and that's why she's here. Her mom couldn't control her, so she sent her to live with her grandparents in Cedar Creek. Just what we need, all the boys trying to get another cute girl to notice them. That won't make her popular with the girls."

One of the freshman girls was already mad at her boyfriend for helping the new girl find her locker. Tanna had offered her assistance when she saw the girl wandering down the hall perusing the locker numbers, but she rebuffed the offer, "Not that dumb, I am. I know numbers."

Tanna had learned to accept the sentence pattern occasionally used by some of her students on the reservation. The wording changed, depending on the situation: "Not that nosy, you are" when someone asked too many questions or "Not that cheesy, she is" when describing a smiling person.

Monica continued and showed no sign of ending her monologue despite Tanna's lack of response.

"And, her aunt is going to move back here, too."

After Tanna briskly shuffled the papers on her desk and pretended to look for something, Monica stood and whispered her last tidbit of gossip before leaving to find someone who would show more enthusiasm for her inside information.

Tanna's thoughts returned to the new girl, and she prayed for a way to set a better tone when she came to class. A wise teacher she'd once known, as well as a few of her own experiences, had made Tanna understand that most students who misbehaved and spat out insolent insults were not angry at her. Their home life was usually the source of their ire, and she was simply the unfortunate beneficiary.

Too soon, the bell rang, and it was time to face the problem. The new girl entered the classroom.

"Welcome to freshman English," Tanna smiled, hoping to put yesterday's animosity behind them.

"Whatever," the new student flicked her long, black hair over her shoulder. Many teachers considered the gesture disrespectful, but Tanna knew she had to pick her battles. This battle was one she couldn't win.

Sliding into an empty desk, the new student immediately turned her attention to the boy closest to her. Tanna placed a piece of paper onto her desk and asked her to please write her name on it.

"With what?" Her sarcastic tone drew snickers from a few nearby students. Concerned she might lose control of the class, Tanna flashed a warning look at the students who knew better than to break her rules. She had worked patiently and consistently with her students since the beginning of the school year to develop an atmosphere of mutual trust and respect. Most of her students knew how far they could go without losing her approval. A few didn't care, and Tanna wondered if she had enough time to draw this troubled girl out of the latter group.

"A pen or pencil—whatever you have." Tanna fought to keep her voice calm and congenial.

The new girl held out her hand to the student beside her. "Got a pencil?"

Tanna slowly walked to the front of the room and lifted two books and a notebook from her desk. By the time she walked back to deposit them on the new girl's desk, she was rewarded with a name scrawled in flowing letters, *Siobhan Lynch*.

Glancing at the paper she held in her hand with the pronunciation of Siobhan's name, Tanna prayed she would pronounce it correctly. This girl seemed ready to erupt at the smallest provocation, and Tanna didn't want to trigger an outburst. She mentally reminded herself it was *Shĭ-vawn*, *before* saying her name out loud.

"Siobhan, we're reading *Romeo and Juliet*; have you read it?"

Her indifferent manner slowly vanished as Siobhan shook her head, and Tanna glimpsed what she thought looked like fear in her luminous brown eyes.

"You've missed the notes for the introduction, but I'll give you a copy of those. Tell me tomorrow if you have any questions." Tanna did her best to calm Siobhan's anxiety by lightly patting her shoulder with her fingertips, noting that the young girl didn't flinch or pull away.

At least I don't think I have to add physical abuse to whatever other traumas she's experienced.

Siobhan's expression quickly transformed from concerned back to uninterested as she averted her eyes and began doodling on her notebook. Tanna had learned to accept downcast eyes from some of her students as a cultural practice, but she struggled with not being able to look directly into their eyes.

Conversations began to erupt among her students, reminding Tanna that there were other students in her classroom and Act I of *Romeo and Juliet* to discuss.

"Billy, what do we know about the Montagues and the Capulets?" Tanna called on her go-to guy, who was always a reliable source for answers to her questions, even if he didn't always have the correct answer.

"The monta-*whose?*" Uproarious laughter caused Billy to give Tanna a sheepish grin.

Trying to stop herself from laughing, Tanna looked around and called on several other students, who either looked down at their books or shook their heads when she called on them. It was obvious that most of the class hadn't read the first act, and those who had didn't want to answer her questions. Even with a modern version of the play included in their book alongside Shakespeare's original words, it still required the willpower to work at understanding what they read. Tanna could explain what they were saying and why they were saying it, but she had to find a way to interest them in the plot if they were ever going to discuss more than just what was happening and to whom.

"Okay, let's try this again. I'll give you the notes, but you'll have to read the assignments, or you won't understand the information we discuss."

Wishing there was a better way, Tanna presented information on the setting, events, and characters in the first act and assigned Act II for Monday.

"You have a little time, so start reading Act II, and you can ask me if you read something you don't understand."

Knowing she had only five or six minutes before her students would give up trying to understand the difficult Shakespearean language, Tanna reviewed the plot for something that would capture their interest.

Suicide was a touchy subject on the reservation, one she didn't feel qualified to address. Many of her students had friends or relatives who had decided life was too much of a struggle to continue, and hanging was the method of choice for most who died deaths as painful as their lives had been. Tanna wondered how many regretted their deadly decision when it was too late to change it.

The class again broke out into chattering groups, and Tanna realized her rapidly wandering thoughts weren't making her search for a way to interest her students very fruitful. She was determined to unravel the play and make it just as memorable for them as it had been for her when she was a freshman student in this classroom all those years ago.

Everybody needs love.

Thank you, Jesus. You always come through for me, even when I forget to ask.

Tanna knew the concept of love was an easy-to-understand theme in *Romeo and Juliet*, and that was what she would use to entice her students to read it

"Shawn, please read the first two lines in the second scene of Act II. This takes place after Romeo and Juliet have met at a party, and then they go their separate ways. Romeo is walking and sees Juliet on her balcony, but she doesn't see or hear him when he says this." Tanna looked at Shawn and nodded.

"'But, soft, what light through yonder window breaks? It is the east, and Juliet is the sun!'"

A few of his classmates snickered, and Shawn turned to Tanna. "That part?"

Tanna nodded and flashed a warning look at one of the laughing students, "What does that mean, Mike?"

His blank look told Tanna he needed a little prompting. "Can you live without the sun?"

"I don't think so."

"Welcome to Romeo's world," Tanna managed to squeeze in just as the bell rang.

Tanna looked at Siobhan as she stood to leave. "I'll give you a copy of those notes if you wait a minute."

After walking to her desk and gathering the notes, Tanna turned, but Siobhan was walking out of the room without a backward glance.

Help me, Lord. Her hurt is deep, and the walls are high.

The second-period class discussion of *Romeo and Juliet* was livelier than the first, but Tanna was surprised when a popular girl asked her if her husband ever said things to her like Romeo said to Juliet.

"No, my husband doesn't speak the language of Shakespeare, if that's what you mean."

"Would you like him to?"

"He tells me he loves me."

"Like how?"

"That's a little too personal for me to answer."

"Then, will you tell me what it's like to be married?"

Knowing that this young student had never known her

father's love or maybe even his name, Tanna hesitated. "It's nice."

"Just nice? Isn't it better than nice to have someone who won't ever leave you?"

Tanna took a deep breath and prayed for an answer that would be truthful without crushing the girl's hopes about marriage.

"Well, I'm not going to tell you it's always easy. There are tough times, but if you're committed to each other, better times eventually come." Tanna hoped her words were true.

CHAPTER TWO

The final bell of the day rang, and Tanna waited to sense the relief she usually felt on Fridays as her last class filed out of the room. Today, she hadn't been able to shake her turbulent feelings after answering her student's marriage question. Why hadn't she painted a more flattering picture? She wanted to believe that there would be more good times, but could she wait for them?

She understood that everything she knew about marriage she had learned from her parents' marriage, not her own. There was an unbreakable connection between Sam and Sarah that she and her brother had never managed to breach, and they had tried when they thought it would give them what they wanted. It was like their parents thought with one mind and one resolve. Tanna longed for that bond with Josh, but she feared the Lord was withholding it because she had not listened to Him when choosing a husband.

There had been frequent tender moments before children and work had monopolized all of their time. The first few years of their marriage had been full of hugs and kisses, flowers and surprises. What had happened to all the good times and sweet love?

The ranch.

That's what had happened. How could something that held so many blissful memories and so much hope, cause this much discontent? Or was she placing the blame in the wrong place? How hard had she really tried to make her marriage work? After making her heart-wrenching choice for a husband, Tanna had expected everything to fall into place. After all, she'd prayed and asked God to guide her.

But had she listened to Him?

"That's the million-dollar question," her dad always said when facing something tricky.

"Oh Daddy, I need your advice. What am I doing wrong? Why can't Josh be more like you?"

Brushing tears from her cheeks, Tanna resolved to ask the only person who could calm her frazzled nerves. She needed a dose of her mom's country wisdom.

Determined to leave at the earliest time allowed by the school administration, Tanna gathered her uncorrected papers and text books and headed for the library where Jaz and Tucker waited for her every day. Many of the teachers were working in their classrooms, which was also Tanna's usual routine. She tried to prepare lessons for the next school day before leaving school because once she reached home, her household and parenting duties left little time for school work.

The librarian spent close to an hour every afternoon putting away books and didn't mind letting Jaz and Tucker read books or play games on one of the computers. Mrs. Philips, her mother's friend, had been the librarian since Tanna was in preschool, and she was really more like another grandmother to Jaz and Tucker.

"Now, if I can just leave here without running into someone who wants to commiserate about the day." Tanna closed and locked her classroom door.

Halfway down the hall, the dean of students, Mrs. Majhor, stepped out of her office and greeted Tanna with a frustrated smile. "How did Siobhan do in your class?"

"Well, she didn't cause any problems, but she didn't seem interested in what we were doing either." Tanna appreciated the woman's sincere interest in the welfare of the students, but she hoped her brief answer wouldn't invite an extended conversation. Not now. Not today.

The attractive Native American woman looked up and down the hall before she responded, "She got into a fight with Tracey Yellow; they'll both be in the detention room for a couple of days, so she'll need her assignments on Monday."

Tanna's shoulders sagged. "Already? Thanks for letting me know. I'll take care of her assignment on Monday."

Tanna turned to leave but stopped when Mrs. Majhor continued, "We need to keep a close watch on her. She's been in and out of a couple of schools and several relatives' homes this year, and she's not too happy about being sent to live with Grandma. Actually, it's not Grandma she objects to; it's Auntie who will make her go to school and monitor her friends and activities."

"Then, it sounds like Auntie is the one I'll call if I have any problems with Siobhan." Tanna understood the dean's concern, but she was distracted by her own problems right now. She once again turned and resolutely walked away after a quick, "Have a nice weekend. See you on Monday."

Tanna found Jaz sitting on the floor and reading a book to Tucker when she walked into the library. The room smelled musty, but it wasn't unpleasant for her. This had been her favorite room when she was a student, and it still brought back pleasant memories every time she stepped in the door. Mrs. Philips often reminded her of her first visit when she was in preschool.

"Oh, look at all these delicious books," Tanna had excitedly told her as she dashed around the room gazing up at the bookshelves.

A weary-looking Mrs. Philips turned and greeted her warmly, "Hello, Tanna."

"Have they been a problem?"

"Oh, no. It's just been a long week, and I think the weather is changing if my kindergarten class is an accurate indication. Those youngsters could go to work for the weather service. Their restless behavior is a better forecaster than radar."

As if on cue, Tucker grabbed the book from Jaz. "You skipped a page! Go back!"

"How do you know? You can't read! Mommy, that's my library book!" Jaz attempted to pry the book from Tucker's clutch.

Tanna rescued the book with an exasperated sigh. "You'll have to finish this on the way home. It's time to go! Now, thank Mrs. Philips and put on your coats."

While her children reluctantly struggled into their coats, Tanna, glanced out the window. "I really hope they're wrong about the weather this time. There are too many baby calves on the ground for a storm, but it's not unusual for them to make their appearance when the weather is the most miserable."

Following her children to the door, Tanna stopped to whisper to them, "Say 'thank you.'"

Jaz turned and grinned, revealing her missing front teeth,

while Tucker ran to Mrs. Philips and wrapped his arms around her waist for a quick hug. "You smell like my Grammy."

"Then, I must smell good." Mrs. Philips patted Tucker's head as he looked up at her.

"Like cookies." Tucker pulled away as Mrs. Philips and Tanna laughed.

"How is your mom?" Concern clouded the librarian's expression.

"I'm worried about her; the last time I saw her, she appeared gaunt and weary. Dad was her whole life, especially after Matt and I moved away. It was really hard for her to move to town after living on the ranch for forty years."

"Sarah loved that ranch." Mrs. Philips pressed her lips together and nodded sympathetically.

"We offered to let her live with us, but she insisted we needed to make the house our own. We're stopping at her house on our way home, and maybe we can convince her to come home with us for the weekend."

"Yes! We're going to Grammy's!" Tucker skipped to the door and suddenly seemed anxious to leave. "Maybe, she has some chocolate chip cookies!"

Jaz crossed her arms and rolled her eyes. "He can be so annoying."

Trying to conceal her surprise, Tanna wondered which of her little friends Jaz was mimicking or if she had come up with that behavior on her own. She made a mental note to talk to her about acting respectfully toward others, even her "annoying" little brother.

Small snippets of blue sky peaked through ominous, gray clouds as the frigid wind propelled them to the car in the staff parking lot behind the school. Tanna quickly unlocked the car doors and rushed her children into their seats. Struggling against the wind, she closed the doors and prayed that this visit to her Mom wasn't too self-serving. Her marital problems seemed minor compared to her Mom's broken heart.

TUCKER BURST into Sarah's bright, spotless kitchen, peeled off his coat, and dropped it on the floor before running across the room. "Grammy, I'm here! Got any cookies?"

"Tucker, I didn't know you were coming today." Sarah turned from her position at the large bay window in her living room.

She often spent her afternoons watching the school children as they passed on their way home from school. Just the sight of bustling young life lifted her spirits on lonely afternoons. Wanting to be a part of something so full of life, she had started praying for them as they walked by her house every day.

Sam had been gone for over a year, but she was still waiting for the grief to ease. Believing she was too blessed to wallow in self-pity, she tried to hide her misery from friends and family. The life Sam created for her had been wonderful, even if it was too short. At sixty, she was young enough to know her life wasn't over because she had buried her husband, but it was a daily struggle to go on without him.

When Sam asked permission to court Sarah, his age hadn't been important to her parents. He was a well-respected rancher who had worked hard and established a sound reputation, making him the most eligible bachelor in Cedar Creek. Despite that, Sarah's parents may not have approved of a man fifteen years older than their daughter if they hadn't seen evidence of his commitment to the Lord in all facets of his life, including his leadership in their church. Sam was the young man every mother hoped would notice her daughter, but he discovered Sarah his way. He told her dad, "When it was time to look for a wife, I sought Jesus, and I found Him standing guard in Sarah's heart."

Reluctantly putting away the treasured memory, Sarah gathered Tucker into a warm hug, "I think there may be one or two cookies for a hungry boy." Turning she opened her arms to embrace Tanna and Jaz. "What a nice surprise."

Tears welled in Sarah's eyes as Tanna snugly wrapped her arms around her mother's slight frame. After a long embrace, Sarah drew back to look into her daughter's tear-filled eyes and followed Tanna's gaze to the table where her scrapbook was open displaying a wedding picture of Sam and Sarah—so young and so in love.

Tucker tilted his head to the side and narrowed his eyes, "How come your eyes are dripping?"

"We're just happy to see each other." Sarah winked at him before wiping her eyes with her apron.

"Mom, we are more than happy to see you. I'm sorry we don't stop by more often."

Sarah turned and walked to the kitchen door, hoping to hide the overwhelming emotions that were rising in her, "I just baked cookies today because I was hoping you'd come."

"We can come for cookies any time you want us to. Right, Mommy?" Sarah noticed Tucker studying Tanna's face.

Tanna nodded encouragingly.

"I know how busy you are, so I'll let you decide when you

have time for a visit." Sarah knew what ranch life was like and didn't want to put any added pressure on her daughter. The truth was she baked a small batch of cookies every day, hoping Tanna and her grandchildren would come. When they didn't, she stored the cookies in the freezer or gave them to her neighbors.

After devouring milk and too many cookies, Tanna asked Tucker and Jaz to take the glasses and napkins to the kitchen.

"No, Mommy, it can't be time to go. We just got here."

"Yeah, and Grammy wants us to stay longer! Please!" Tucker put on his best beggar face.

Sarah sensed that her daughter had something on her mind, but she obviously didn't want to talk about it in front of her children.

Noticing the dark sky, Sarah's protective instincts prompted her to send her family on their way as quickly as possible. "I'd love to have you stay, but it's dark outside, and you have a long drive home. Maybe you can stay longer next time."

"Why don't you come home with us for the weekend, Mom." Tanna's abrupt question surprised Sarah.

"Yay! I can show you my new rope trick!" Tucker spun an imaginary rope above his head.

"And I could read my library book to you. Teacher says we're supposed to practice reading at home, and Mommy and Daddy are always too busy to listen." Jaz wriggled under Sarah's arm giving her a pleading look.

"Mom, we haven't had a good talk for a long time, and you could bring your scrapbook. It's been a long time since I've seen those old pictures."

Indecision clouded Sarah's face, "We're having a pot

blessing dinner in church on Sunday, and there are so few of us—I don't want to miss it."

"I could bring you into town early Sunday morning before we go to church," Tanna assured her.

Tanna and Josh had joined a nondenominational church in a nearby town after returning to Cedar Creek, but Sarah remained with the church her family had attended for years. Sarah understood their need for fellowship with other young families, but she missed interacting with her grandchildren on Sunday mornings. Tanna had invited her to their new church, but it was too contemporary for Sarah who preferred singing familiar hymns and worshipping in the church where she had met and married Sam.

Sarah drew in a long breath and released it. "But I won't have anything prepared for the dinner."

"We have a kitchen where you know your way around very well and a freezer full of meat and vegetables. I'm sure you can find something to make, can't you, Mom?"

Tucker couldn't resist adding one more incentive. "We'll help you cook, Grammy. Except Daddy probably won't. Mommy gets mad at him when he doesn't help."

Sarah noticed the worried look on Tucker's face as he shifted his sideways glance to his mom who was frowning. Sarah knew Tanna's family followed the same rule she and Sam had imposed on their children to keep what they heard at home to themselves. Sensing her daughter's embarrassment, Sarah agreed to go home with them but said she needed to pack her bag.

Worried that he had broken the family rule to not talk too much about what he heard at home, Tucker gave Tanna a tentative glance, but she was too absorbed with helping

Sarah to notice. Fifteen minutes later, they walked to the car with their heads bent against the icy wind.

Before leaving town, they stopped to buy a pizza for supper at the gas station convenience store. Tanna maneuvered the car onto the road toward home as the sleet began to fall.

CHAPTER THREE

Taking one more anxious look down the driveway, Josh entered his dark house and wondered again why Tanna wasn't home from school yet. Mentally, he checked the list of possible reasons for their delay: Tanna was taking tickets at a basketball game? No, the season ended last weekend. A music concert at the school? No, too early for that. Parent-teacher conferences? No, they were last month. Some kind of event for Jaz or Tucker? No, Tanna would have reminded him this morning. Something going on at church? No, again, Tanna would have reminded him. Where were they?

Checking the answering machine with no results, he gave in to the frustration that seemed to be his constant companion. Tanna knew better than to be out on a night like this. Hadn't she checked on the weather forecast? He had enough on his mind with ten new calves on the ground and twenty-five heifers ready to drop their calves any day.

Changes in the weather often brought about an onslaught of early births, and the first-calf heifers weren't always the most vigilant about finding a sheltered place to protect their offspring from the brutal South Dakota wind and snow of a spring storm. The baby calves were wet and needed their mamas to lick them dry before the wind chilled their body temperatures beyond their ability to survive. The calves that lived often lost the tips of their ears due to frostbite which lowered their value at market.

Josh had spent most of the day herding the heifers closer to home and putting those that looked closest to calving into the barn, but it was often nothing more than a good guess which deliveries were imminent. He'd be up several times during the night to check on them, but that didn't always guarantee success. Last year, five calves had died despite his best efforts. When they were working on a profit margin as slim as theirs, there wasn't much room for mistakes.

Regardless of his concern for the cattle, his first responsibility was his family. He accepted that. They were the reason he worked so hard to make a go of it on the ranch. If it was Tanna's dream, it was his dream, and he would make it come true—one way or another. Lately, their relationship had been strained, and he knew that, but he didn't have time to fix it now.

Why not now?

Okay, I'm not ready to tell her everything, he answered the voice in his heart, *and I'll make it right. Just bring her home. Keep her safe, please.*

Josh cast another worried glance out of the kitchen window and breathed a sigh of relief when he saw headlights turning into the driveway. The sleet that started an hour ago was mixed with snow now, and the wind whipped it across the driveway, momentarily obscuring the headlights. The snow squall appeared to part as the car inched along and slid to a stop just short of the garage door.

Tempted to dash out and embrace his family in a jubilant group hug, Josh instead pulled on his coat and bowed his head against the frigid blast of wet snow that hit him as he lifted open the garage door. Tucker and Jaz jumped out of the car, ignoring Tanna's objections, and ran toward Josh, anxious to escape the blowing snow that caught on their shoulders and clung to their eyelashes.

"Grammy is here," Tucker informed Josh as he slipped by him in the doorway. With a resigned sigh, Josh turned up his collar and stepped out of the way so Tanna could drive into the garage.

―――

TANNA WAS LOST in thought as her family ate their pizza and a hastily prepared lettuce salad. She couldn't stop thinking about having some private time with her mom, and she hoped Josh was too preoccupied with the weather to try to draw her into the table conversation.

It was warm and cozy around the kitchen table, but the ruthless wind was spinning an opaque wall between the house and the barn. Some of the pregnant cows were in the barn, and Josh said he wanted to check on them, so he bundled up to go out in the storm after he finished eating. Tucker insisted that he could help, but Josh convinced him that he should relax for now in case he needed his help later.

Sarah cleared the dishes while Tanna found a family-friendly adventure movie on Netflix for Jaz and Tucker to watch. They nestled into their blankets on the couch, and Tanna went to the kitchen to make tea. "Mom, let's look at your pictures."

Sarah retrieved her old photo album from the bedroom she had shared with Sam which was now the guest room.

She joined Tanna at the dining room table, and they were soon laughing and reminiscing over the old photos.

"Mom, how did you talk Grandpa into wearing a tuxedo? He looks kind of uncomfortable."

"It wasn't the tuxedo that caused his pained expression; he often wore suits to church. It was the picture-taking he didn't like."

Tanna turned the page of the photo album. "Taking pictures didn't seem to bother you and Dad. Your smile fills your whole face, and Dad can't take his eyes off you." The picture of the beaming young couple filled Sarah's face with a fusion of pleasure and sadness, and Tanna waited for Sarah's pensive expression to fade before she asked, "What was your secret?"

"Secret?"

Sarah's furrowed brow prompted Tanna to hesitantly continue, "...To the perfect marriage you and Dad had."

Sarah studied her daughter's face. "What makes you think it was perfect?"

"Well, wasn't it?"

Tilting her head slightly, Sarah searched Tanna's face. "What's this about?"

Before Tanna could respond, the tea kettle whistled. As she poured hot water into their cups, Tanna pondered how to answer her mother without revealing the depth of her cynicism about her own marriage.

"I'm curious how you and Dad made a happy marriage look so easy. You lived on this ranch and were just as busy as Josh and I are. Dad took care of the ranch while you worked at the bank every day, but you always seemed to have time for each other."

Accepting the cup of tea, Sarah studied Tanna. "We did

have fun, but you were not always aware that keeping this ranch afloat was anything but fun."

"No, I knew there were some rough times, but you and Dad were connected. You were like one person. Matt and I could never play you against each other."

Without warning, the lights flickered on and off two times before leaving the house completely dark and quiet until the silence was pierced by Jaz's scream.

"Mommy, where are you?" Jaz whimpered into the inky darkness that surrounded her.

"Stay with your brother, Jaz. I'll be there as soon as I find a flashlight," Tanna called out before cautiously feeling her way along the furniture and walls into the kitchen to find the drawer that she hoped still held a flashlight.

Quickly rummaging through the contents, her hand closed around cool metal, and she pressed the button, praying the batteries weren't dead. The beam was dim, but she made her way into the living room where Jaz and Tucker were huddled on the sofa, their wide eyes threatening to spill the tears that had collected.

"The electricity just went off. It will probably be back on soon," she soothed her children, wrapping her arms around them.

"It was really dark, Mommy. I told Jaz she could hold my hand and we could pray." Tucker proudly awaited Tanna's approval.

"Good job, Bud." Tanna tightened her arm around him.

"But we didn't pray." Jaz folded her arms not wanting to be left out.

"Then, let's pray now." Tanna tightened her hold on Jaz, too.

"May I join you?" Sarah entered the room carrying her cell phone with the flashlight turned on.

"Mom. I'm sorry I left you alone in the dark."

"I just had to find my purse, and I still know my way around this house—even in the dark."

"Sit by me, Grammy." Tucker nudged Tanna to move, and Sarah settled into the space between her daughter and grandson.

They closed their eyes, and Tanna began, "Jesus, being in the dark can be scary, but we know we never have to be afraid because You will never leave us and Your love shines light into a dark world. Thank You for loving us and bringing us safely to our warm home. Protect those who are traveling tonight. In your precious name we…"

"And please protect Daddy and the calves out in the storm. Amen." Tucker added with his folded hands pressed against his tightly closed eyes.

Embarrassed for not remembering to pray for Josh, Tanna assured Tucker, "Daddy is always really careful, and he's good at taking care of the calves, honey. They'll be all right."

The phone rang, and Tanna walked to the kitchen with her flashlight, thankful they had kept a corded telephone with their landline when they moved into the house. She spoke briefly to one of their neighbors who was checking to see if their power was also off. She had reported it to the electric company, and she agreed to keep in touch if she heard anything about the cause of the outage or how long it would last. Tanna thanked her and hung up the phone.

Opening a few drawers and cupboard doors in search of more flashlights or candles, Tanna found a box of matches and two decorative Christmas candles. She lit them and placed one on the kitchen table and carried the other into the living room. Jaz and Tucker were cuddled with Sarah under a blanket on the couch, and she was telling them about Matt and Tanna when they were young children.

"I always thought your mom did whatever her brother told her to do, but I think your mom talked her brother into this scheme. When your Uncle Matt was about eight and your mom was six, they built a big snowman and decided to bring it in the house to surprise me. It was a warm sunny day in March, I think, and I let them play outside after they bundled up in their snow pants and parkas. I was in the basement doing the laundry when I heard them walking across the kitchen floor. I didn't want them to track snow on my clean kitchen floor, so I called up to remind them to leave their boots in the garage. They both started giggling, and I knew something was going on when I heard a chair being dragged across the floor."

"Mom! Not that story again. How many times have you told them about the melting snowman sitting at the kitchen table?" Tanna shook her head, but her smile was good-natured.

They all turned toward the kitchen when they heard the door creak open and footsteps walking across the kitchen floor.

"Maybe Daddy is sneaking a snowman into the house, Grammy." Laughter followed Tucker as he took off for the kitchen.

The low murmur of Josh's voice blended with the excited pitch of Tucker's voice drifted into the living room where Tanna waited, snuggly wrapped in blankets. The phone rang, and Tucker returned to his place between Sarah and Tanna.

"Daddy's talking on the phone. I think it's Jim because

Daddy said, 'Hey, Jim. How are our neighbors doing?' We don't have any other 'Jim' neighbors, do we?"

"I'm sure it's our 'Jim' neighbor because his wife called earlier. I hope they have some news about the electricity." Tanna strained to listen but could only hear her husband's occasional "uh huh" and "really?"

"Mommy, Daddy said the cows and calves in the barn are warm and dry."

Jaz turned to look at her brother. "The cows don't all fit in the barn. What about *them*?"

Tanna was sure Josh had left out that detail when he talked to Tucker because he didn't want him to worry. It would be a frigid night for the outside cows and calves, but nothing could be done about it now.

"The electrical outage could go on for days, but they don't really know," Josh announced when he walked into the room. "Some of the older electrical poles toppled under the weight of ice-encased power lines so it will be a cold night. I'm going to move this recliner into the kitchen because I'll have to add wood to the fire during the night, or our water lines could freeze."

"That's why Sam installed that wood burning stove years ago. He always added wood to the stove before he went to check the cows at night during calving season. Then it was toasty warm when he came back in from the cold."

Sarah's contented smile told Tanna her mom relished the memory.

"How can we be toasty warm in our rooms, Grammy? The wood stove doesn't heat the whole house." Jaz pulled her blanket up to her chin.

"The propane fireplace here in the living room will

provide some heat for my bedroom, but it will be a chilly night."

"Can I sleep with Grammy to keep her warm?" Jaz looked from Tanna to Sarah.

Tanna suspected her daughter was worried about sleeping without a nightlight, but it sounded like a good idea so she looked at Sarah for approval.

"I have to warn you that I snore, but I'll keep you warm."

"No worries Grammy, I hear Daddy snoring all the time when he takes a nap." Jaz grinned at Josh.

"Let's go warm up our bed then. Which side do you want?"

Tanna followed them to the bedroom with her flashlight to make sure they had enough blankets. When she returned to the living room, Josh was adding wood to the fire before he settled into his recliner, and Tucker was asleep on the couch. Tanna decided that would be her bed for the night, too, because she didn't want her brave little son to wake in the dark and not know where he was. Drifting off to sleep in the eerily quiet house, she prayed for the comforting sounds of electricity to wake her in the morning.

CHAPTER FOUR

Total stillness greeted Tanna as the dim rays of sunlight filtered into the living room. All the morning sounds that had become commonplace were noticeably absent. There was no humming coming from the refrigerator or hot water heater. The whir of the ceiling fan and the whoosh of warm air flowing through the floor vents were silent.

She untangled herself from Tucker and flexed her shoulders and arms to relieve her cramped muscles. Her shivering son had nestled into her arms in the middle of the night, keeping her awake until the early hours of the morning.

Walking into the bathroom and automatically flipping the light switch to no avail reminded Tanna again there was no electricity, and without electricity there was no running water.

She smiled when she saw the pail of water on the bathroom floor. Josh must have carried it in from outside this morning. They would need it to fill the tank on the stool so they could flush after everyone was up.

I really do have a thoughtful husband. As soon as she thought it, she stubbornly amended it by adding, *sometimes.*

Shaking her head, Tanna resolved to discard her conflicting emotions about Josh for now. There was no time this morning to figure out what was wrong with her marriage. She shivered as she walked into her cold bedroom and quickly dressed in her warmest sweater, leggings, and socks. The world outside her window revealed snow heaped in huge, lopsided piles everywhere, but at least the snow and wind had ended their vicious assault.

Tanna expected Josh to be in the kitchen, but she found an empty recliner with his blanket draped across the seat. The heat radiating from the stove meant he had recently added wood to the fire. *He must be outside checking the cows and putting gas in the little generator. Why did I let him talk me out of buying a bigger generator? Electricity for the house would make everything so much easier right now.*

Standing as close as she could to the hot stove, she soaked in the warmth that was distinct to wood fires. It seemed to warm something deep within her before radiating to the outside of her flesh. Drawn to the recliner, Tanna slipped under the blanket and gathered it to her face inhaling her husband's familiar scent. She imagined Josh's touch as she caught a faint whiff of his spicy after shave.

I find comfort and safety in his arms. He's what I wanted. Isn't he? She'd asked herself that question too many times since moving back to Cedar Creek. Her husband said he loved her, and she adored their little family.

Then why do I want more?

Her eyes roamed the room and landed on a plaque friends had given them for a wedding gift. It was artfully engraved with their names and the words "Love Never Fails" forming a perfect circle around a cross. Tanna had hung it with boundless expectation when they moved to the ranch. She thought God was giving them a chance to build a marriage like her parents had. *But what if there had never been love? What if I chose the wrong man?*

You are loved with an everlasting love.

I know you love me, Lord, but I need my husband's love and attention.

Leaning her head against the back of the recliner, she stared at the ceiling, and tears quickly gathered. One tear was making the slow trek down the side of her cheek when she heard a sleepy voice. "Mommy, I'm hungry."

Swiping away her tears with the back of her hand, Tanna sat up and turned away from Tucker's quizzical look.

"How about some pancakes?" Before he had a chance to look more closely at her, she stood and walked to the pantry.

"First, I have to wash my hands, but there's no water in the faucet—not the hot or the cold." Tucker waved his hands, palms up and fingers splayed.

Tanna put the ingredients on the counter and lifted the tea kettle from the kitchen range, jiggling it to gauge the amount of water it held. "Without electricity, the pump can't bring any water into the house, so the faucets won't have any water. I'll pour this water in the sink so you can wash your hands, but don't drain it when you finish. We have to conserve water, so you can't flush the stool every time either."

"But Mommy, you said we're supposed to flush every time."

"I know, Sweetie, but that's when we have electricity."

"Okay, but I already flushed." Tucker cocked his head to one side and peeked at Tanna through squinted eyes.

Tanna kissed the top of his head. "That's all right. Just remember next time."

"You're saying we can't ever flush again?" Tanna smiled at the incredulous look on Tucker's face.

"Daddy will bring some water in so we can fill the tank on the stool and flush it."

Tucker squinted his eyes suspiciously. "Where will he get water, and where did the water in the tea kettle come from?"

"Daddy connected the little generator to the pump outside so the cattle can have water. He will dip some out of the tank and bring it in the house, and the water in the tea kettle is left over from last night when Grammy and I had tea."

Tucker pondered her answer and then moved to the desk beside the pantry. "Maybe we should put a sign in the bathroom so Grammy and Jaz won't flush." Tucker opened the drawer that held colored pencils and paper. "But I don't know how to write all those words."

"How about if I write the words on the sign, and you can color it while I make pancakes."

"Sure, but you better hurry. I heard Jaz talking to Grammy a little while ago."

"Well then, why don't you just go in and tell them while I make breakfast?"

Tanna was opening the refrigerator when Tucker rushed back into the kitchen. "Mommy, guess what."

"What?" Tanna didn't wait for an answer but quickly took the eggs out of the refrigerator and closed the door so she wouldn't lose too much of the precious cold air that remained inside. She had to think of something before everything spoiled. She could put the frozen food outside, but what could she do to keep the milk and eggs cold without freezing them?

Tucker moved closer to Tanna and touched her arm to

get her attention "Grammy says we should melt snow for our water. Can I go get some right now?"

"Yes!" Tanna beamed at Tucker. "That's what we need. Snow! We can put our food in an ice chest with snow to keep it cold."

Tanna laughed at Tucker's wide eyes and open mouth. "You and Jaz can bring in lots of snow after breakfast. Now, set the table."

After breakfast, Sarah insisted on helping Tucker and Jaz gather snow to melt. Tanna briefly forgot the difficult situation they were facing as the three excitedly left the kitchen with their pails and kettles. Her mother made it seem like they were going on a great adventure. Tucker and Jaz had only begun to experience the primitive conditions they were facing.

"How bad is it?" Tanna scooped up the last pancakes from the cast iron skillet on the woodburning stove as Josh wearily lowered himself onto a chair at the kitchen table.

"It's not good, but it could be worse." Josh raked his hand over his face. "The storm came up before I had a chance to herd all the cows closer to home. We lost two of the heifers' calves last night. One was completely covered with snow before I found it. The mama was wandering around bellering for her calf, so I went looking, but it was too late."

Defeat was written across his face as he met Tanna's concerned look. "She was one I didn't expect to have a calf for at least a week, so I didn't try to put her in the barn. Well, I did, but she wouldn't cooperate. Stubborn cow!" Josh slammed his fist on the table, causing Tanna to jump.

"You did what you could, Josh."

"It wasn't enough. Do you think your dad would have lost those calves?"

"He lost more than that the year Matt was born." Sarah lugged a pail of snow into the kitchen.

"Mom, I didn't hear you come in." Tanna took the pail from Sarah and looked behind her. "Where are Tucker and Jaz?"

"They think it's fun to make snowballs and throw them into their kettles, but mostly, they're throwing them at each other. It's cold out, so they'll be in soon."

Sarah turned her attention to Josh as she took off her coat. "Now, as for Sam losing calves, he lost twelve calves a few days after we brought Matt home from the hospital. It was a storm like last night that started with rain and turned into a snow storm. No one expected it; we thought winter was over. Sam was so discouraged he threatened to give up ranching and look for a job in town."

"That's not a bad idea," Josh conceded just before Jaz and Tucker burst into the kitchen.

Tanna blocked her rosy-cheeked children from walking too far into the kitchen and steered them back to the garage to help them remove their snow encrusted clothes and boots. Tanna strained to hear what her mother and husband were saying over Jaz and Tucker's excited chatter. It was only apparent that the two adults were having a serious conversation. Tanna had just pulled the last, snowy leg of Tucker's snowsuit off when Josh stepped into the garage.

"Daddy, look at all the snow that me and Jaz got to make water!"

"You did a great job. Now you can help Grammy melt it." Josh took his insulated coveralls off the hook by the door.

"Can I go with you, Daddy? It's not too cold for me. Jaz was shivering, but I wasn't."

"Not this time, Little Man. I don't know how long I'll be

gone." Josh didn't know if there were more dead calves in the pasture, and he didn't want Tucker to experience that.

Tucker watched hopefully from the kitchen as Josh donned his winter gear. Maybe his dad would change his mind if he didn't beg or whine, but it didn't seem promising.

"Maybe I can go next time," Tucker murmured as Josh pulled his hood over his head.

"Maybe you can," Josh winked at Tucker before opening the outside door.

"Pete!" Josh was startled to find his neighbor standing in the doorway.

Pete White Owl extended his hand to shake Josh's hand and smiled broadly. "Can a neighbor get a cup o' hot coffee?"

"Sure, but I'm on my way out to the north pasture. I didn't hear you drive up. Where's your pickup?" Josh stepped away from the door to let Pete enter.

"I had to park on the road. There's an electric pole busted across your driveway. I heard on the radio that over a hundred poles are down across the county. Out here in the country, we're gonna be without juice for a couple weeks."

"A couple weeks? Really? I wonder what they'll do about school?"

"On the radio, they said Cedar Creek has electricity, so there will be school unless the roads are blocked."

"Then, we're going to have to figure out a way for Tanna and the kids to get to town. How are you and Millie doing? Are you keeping warm?"

"Oh yeah. I have a generator so we're doin' just fine. Burnin' a lot of gas, though. The radio said another storm might be movin' in tonight. That's why I came over here to see if you need anything before it storms again." Before Josh turned to leave, he leaned close and spoke quietly to

Pete. The two men shook hands again, and Josh went outside.

"Come in and warm up by the stove." Tanna hugged Pete after taking his coat. He'd been a good friend of her dad's since high school, and she considered him and Millie a part of their family.

"I remember when Sam put that stove in here. I told him he was takin' a step back in time, but I think he knew what he was doin'. It's a lot cheaper to burn wood than gas." Pete stretched his hands over the stove and let loose his full-throated, hearty laugh.

Sarah cautiously approached Pete in the large kitchen. She hadn't seen him since Sam's funeral, and when he mentioned Sam, her emotions had risen to the surface. "Pete, it's good to see you," she managed to say in an even tone, but when Pete enfolded her in a hug, they both struggled to maintain control.

Wiping her eyes, Sarah pulled away after patting Pete's back. "Thanks to Sam, we'll be warm, but it'll be dark after the sun goes down."

"Come on over to our house. Millie would be happy for the company—especially those two little ones of yours, Tanna."

"Pete, if my grandchildren go anywhere, it will be to my house in town. You said the electricity was still on there, didn't you?"

"Sarah," Pete said in that slow, drawn out way of his as he smiled broadly at her. "Don't get your dander up. I'm just bein' neighborly. Millie would think it was Christmas day if all of you came home with me."

"Thanks, Pete, but if the electricity will be off for two weeks, I think we should stay with Mom in town. It'll be easier to go to school from there." Tanna interrupted the banter between Sarah and Pete as she set mugs of steaming coffee on the table.

"I'll take you to town, then. Nobody's gettin' in or out of your driveway with that pole across it." Pete looked from Sarah to Tanna for confirmation that his offer was being accepted.

"How soon do we have to be ready? I'll have to talk to Josh before we leave." Tanna suddenly felt conflicted about leaving Josh to fend for himself.

"Josh already asked me to take all of you to town. He said it would be one less thing for him to worry about, and I'll check on him tonight for you. Don't worry."

Reluctantly, Tanna went to break the news to Jaz and Tucker that they were moving to town. She knew Tucker would protest, but she'd have to be firm with him.

In less than an hour, Pete, Sarah, Tanna, and the children were walking to the end of the driveway pulling a sled piled with their suitcases. Tanna glanced back at the house she and Josh shared and contemplated how she could have so many ambivalent feelings. Maybe her mom could help her sort it all out.

CHAPTER FIVE

On the trip to town, Pete and Sarah kept up a lively conversation, recalling past snow storms, and Jaz excitedly questioned Tanna about staying in town. "Can I invite my friends over after school?"

"Let's wait a few days until Grammy adjusts to our bedlam before we add to it. Okay, Honey?

"I should have stayed home with Daddy. Jaz will invite all those girls over, and they won't play with me." Tucker pouted. "What will Daddy do without us, Mommy?"

"Daddy will have the new calves to keep him busy. Don't worry—he can take care of himself."

"But you always say…" Tucker folded his arms and squinted at Tanna. "'I don't know what that man would do without me.'"

Tanna anxiously checked if Pete and Sarah had heard Tucker's remark but was relieved that they were still engaged in their own friendly banter.

"I just mean that Daddy and I make a good team. I do the things he forgets to do." Tanna hoped that explanation would satisfy her inquisitive son. "Don't worry."

Even a four-year-old can spot the problems in our marriage. Tanna didn't want her frustration to be obvious to her children, and the last thing she wanted was for them to carry her burden.

I'll do that if you let Me.

"I know." The unbidden words interrupted the momentary silence before Tanna could stop them.

"What do you know, dear?" Sarah turned to look into the back seat.

Tanna's eyes widened. "I'm just talking to myself, Mom."

"She does that a lot." Tucker's head bobbed as Tanna laughed to hide her embarrassment.

"And this one always makes fun of me." Tanna tickled her son's ribs and wrapped her arm around him. "What do you want to do at Grammy's house?

"I want to have cookies every day." He looked hopefully at Sarah.

"We might be able to make that happen." Sarah smiled contentedly. "Maybe we can talk Pete and Millie into coming for a visit, too." Tanna eyed her mom's countenance, hopeful that the sorrow she carried was lightening—at least for now.

"We'll have to do that. Millie gets awful lonesome, and you know me—I'm not much of a talker."

"Since when?"

"Since Millie decided we need to talk about our feelings. Why does an old man like me have to start talkin' about how he feels?"

"Because your wife needs to hear it." Tanna cut into the conversation.

"She should know how I feel after all these years. I'll let her know if anything changes."

"Sometimes a wife just needs to hear the words one more time," Sarah softly added.

Pete gave Sarah a perceptive glance. "I miss him, too." He touched her arm as he turned into her driveway.

WITH HER GRANDCHILDREN on her heels, Sarah trudged through the snow piled against the garage door. She unlocked the door, and Jaz and Tucker raced into the house flipping every light switch.

"The lights work, Grammy." Jaz beamed as Sarah and Tanna helped Pete carry the suitcases into the kitchen.

Tucker darted from the bathroom into the kitchen. "So does the water."

"Well, looks like you're all set. Let me know if you need anything." Pete set the last suitcase on the floor and turned to leave.

"Thanks, Pete. Would you mind checking on Josh tomorrow? Unless it's storming again," Tanna added as she hugged him and opened the door.

"Thank you and give Millie a hug." Sarah called out before Pete closed the door.

Sarah had two extra bedrooms, and Tanna helped her children carry their suitcases to the room with the bunk beds. Jaz would sleep on the top and Tucker on the bottom bunk. At first, Tucker protested that Jaz got the top bunk, but Tanna pointed out that the bottom bed had cowboy sheets and the sheets on top were pink.

The bunk beds had been in Matt's room when they lived on the ranch, but Sarah purchased new sheets when she moved the beds to town. Guilt overcame Tanna as she realized this was only the second time they had slept at her mom's house since she'd moved to town. Why had she let their lives become too busy to have time for her mom? Looking back over the year, she couldn't think of anything meaningful she had accomplished. Surely, there was more to life than merely existing.

Ask Me, I'll show you.

Tanna shook off her inner turmoil and helped Jaz and Tucker unpack their suitcases. She closed the closet door and directed her children to find their grandmother. "Ask her if she needs help with anything. I'll be there as soon as I unpack my suitcase."

―――――

TUCKER CAME BOUNDING into the kitchen followed closely by Jaz. "Do you need any help, Grammy?"

Sarah opened the refrigerator door. "Is anybody hungry? I could make an omelet."

"And then can we have cookies?"

"Not tonight, honey, or your mom may decide to pack up and leave."

"I don't think we have to worry about that, Grammy. She's unpacking everything so she'll be too tired to put it all back into the suitcase." Tucker's sly grin made Sarah smile.

"Let's save the cookies for tomorrow. Now, let's see; I have mushrooms, green peppers, onion, and cheese. Do you like all of those?"

"Eww!" Both of her grandchildren squealed and then laughed as they faced each other. Jaz scrunched up her nose. "We hate mushrooms."

"Okay, no mushrooms for the lady and gentleman. Anything else you don't want in your omelet?"

"No yucky broccoli." Tucker giggled.

"Only yummy broccoli in Tucker's omelet." Sarah pretended to write on the palm of her hand.

The kitchen was filled with laughter when Tanna entered. "What's so funny in here? Are you two being helpful or making extra work for Grammy?

"Grammy is making omelets for us. You don't like mushrooms." Tucker's forehead wrinkled. "Or do you?"

"I love mushrooms!" Tanna ran her hand across Tucker's head. "Mom, do you need some help?"

Sarah looked up from the stove. "Jaz and Tucker's omelet is ready if you want to divide it for them. I'll make one for us with mushrooms. There's juice and milk in the refrigerator if anyone wants it."

After his first bite, Tucker declared Sarah's omelet "the best ever" but added, "Mommy doesn't normally make eggs for supper, and she's too busy in the morning."

"Mommy, Tucker's talking about what we do at home again." Jaz flashed a half smile at Tucker.

"Jaz, Daddy and I don't want you to talk about personal things to people who aren't part of our family. Do you understand what personal things are?"

Tucker narrowed his eyes. "You mean like when Daddy walks around in his underwear?"

"Well, yes." Tanna laughed. "You don't need to tell everyone that he walks around in his underwear, but what we really don't want you to do is repeat something you hear when we're talking privately. You may not understand what we mean, so don't repeat it. Okay?" Jaz and Tucker nodded their agreement.

"But what if I forget?"

"Just try your best to remember, Tucker. Now, it's time for both of you to go to bed."

"Grammy, will you read us a story?" Jaz and Tucker each held one of Sarah's hands.

"Mom, go ahead if you don't mind. I'll clean up the kitchen and check in with Josh."

TANNA HAD JUST FINISHED her phone conversation with her husband when Sarah came into the living room. "Josh said to thank you for bringing the snow into the house to melt before you left. He was happy to already have water in the house after he checked the cows."

"Did he say how the cows are doing?"

"He found one more dead calf, but he managed to get all the cows closer to shelter in case another storm comes. He sounded really tired." Tanna paused and lowered her gaze to her hands. "I have to ask you a question."

Sarah waited for her daughter to continue. The only sound in the room came from the second hand ticking its way around the face of the wall clock.

"Did you ever think you married the wrong man?"

Sarah thought for a moment. "No, not really. At first our age difference limited the friends we socialized with because all the young men my friends were married to or dating didn't have much in common with Sam. Frankly, they seemed immature compared to him, but it became less obvious as we all aged." Sarah studied Tanna before adding, "Why do you ask?"

"Mom, you must already know that things aren't right with me and Josh. You're too perceptive not to notice." When Sarah didn't respond, Tanna continued, "Sometimes, I think I chose the wrong man. What if God didn't tell me to marry my Josh?"

"I think you just answered your question."

Tanna's puzzled expression prompted Sarah to continue. "You said 'my Josh,' and I think that's the way God sees this. You married him; he's your husband forever."

"But Josh isn't anything like the man I thought I was marrying. I don't know if he's changed or if I have, but sometimes I think I'm living with a stranger." Tanna couldn't hold back her tears as she covered her face with her hands.

"Oh, sweetheart, has Josh done anything to hurt you?" Sarah reached out and gathered her weeping daughter into an embrace.

Tanna drew away and shook her head. "No, Mom, not physically. And he hasn't been unfaithful, either. We just don't connect anymore. I've tried telling him, but nothing changes."

"Have you prayed about it?"

"All the time, but my prayers just seem to evaporate into the air. I don't know what to do, and it sounds like you think I just have to live with it."

Sarah fingered the button on the cuff of her sleeve for a few moments before fixing her troubled eyes on Tanna. "Have you had any contact with…the other Josh?"

"No! He's married, and I would never try to break up a marriage. Mom, please tell me you don't think I'd do that."

Tanna's sharp answer caused Sarah to draw back. "Oh, Sweetie, I didn't mean to accuse you of anything. I just thought maybe your paths had crossed sometime recently. I'm trying to understand what you want, Tanna. If you think it was a mistake to marry Josh, do you want a divorce?"

"I want… I want Josh to care about my happiness, to

want to meet my needs, to try to understand me. Is that too much to ask?" Tanna covered her face with her hands and sobbed.

Sarah wrapped her arms around Tanna and cradled her while their tears flowed unhindered. Caressing her daughter's back, Sarah waited for her daughter's tears to ebb before telling her how much she loved her and wanted her to be happy.

"I love you, too, Mom. Now, it's time for me to go to bed. Jaz and Tucker don't usually let me sleep very late on Sunday morning. What time does church start?"

"How would you like to be able to sleep until you wake up tomorrow?"

Tanna cocked her head and gave her mother a curious look. "We'll go to church with you. Or do you want to stay home?"

"Let me double check, but I think church was cancelled." Sarah scrolled through the messages on her phone. "I thought I saw something when I came back from putting Jaz and Tucker to bed. Here it is. 'No church due to the weather conditions.' It's from the pastor's wife. I guess we'll have church right here tomorrow. I'll make breakfast, and you can sleep as late as you want. The kids and I can read some Bible storybooks until you're ready to watch an online service with us."

"Thanks, Mom. Good night." Tanna gave Sarah a quick hug, but before she left, Sarah grasped Tanna's hands and held them against her heart.

"I don't believe God desires any of His children to be unhappy. If I could give you the key to a perfect marriage, I would, but there is one truth I believe with all my heart: Even if God may not have written your love story, it doesn't mean He can't make it right. Do you want Him to make it right?"

"I don't know, Mom. Yes... if Josh changes back into the man I married. If he doesn't, I..." Tanna shrugged her shoulders.

Sarah hesitated for a moment and then earnestly looked at Tanna. "You have to want it to work, honey. Remember when Dad gave Matt a bottle calf right after his ninth birthday? He told him if he took good care of it, he could keep the money when we sold the calves in the fall?"

Tanna nodded but then tilted her head questioningly. "You didn't think it was fair and insisted that you were old enough to have your own bottle calf, too." Sarah raised her eyebrows until Tanna once again nodded her head. "The next day, one of the cows had twins and wouldn't claim one of them. Dad asked if you really thought you could do the job. It wasn't easy. You had to mix up the milk replacer, wash out the bottle at least two times every day, and make sure your calf had fresh water and a clean area. That was the hardest part for you."

Tanna still looked puzzled but added that she remembered how hard it was as the calf got bigger and really butted his head around when he was sucking on the bottle. "He almost knocked me over until I learned to brace myself against something solid. I was happy when I could just make sure it had a supply of feed and fresh water.

"But do you remember how determined you were to make sure your calf was as well cared for as Matt's?"

"Yes... What are you getting at, Mom?"

"Did your calf always cooperate?"

"No, but I still don't..." Tanna closed her eyes and bowed her head. "My calf had a stubborn streak, and sometimes, I wanted to give up on him, but Mom, he was an animal and didn't care how I felt."

"Oh, Tanna, I know, but my point is you wanted to succeed, so you didn't give up. Maybe it's not the best example, but it's all I could come up with this late at night."

Tanna gave her mom a one-armed hug before walking away. "You've given me a lot to think about. I'm not sure I'll be able to fall asleep, so don't let me sleep too late in the morning."

Tanna left the room and cautiously opened the door to her children's room, but Jaz and Tucker were sleeping soundly. After covering Tucker with his cast-off blanket, Tanna whispered a quick prayer for her children and quietly left the room. She brushed her teeth and washed her face, all the while hoping she would be able to find a Bible in her mom's guest room. She didn't want to admit that she hadn't given a thought to taking her Bible when she packed her suitcase. She was ashamed to admit that she seldom opened her Bible except on Sundays in church.

After going to her bedroom and slipping into a nightgown, Tanna opened one of the nightstand drawers. She smiled when she saw the items her meticulous mother had deemed necessary for her guests. There were throat lozenges, a small bottle of lotion, a new toothbrush, toothpaste, and some dental floss.

Sliding to the other side of the bed, Tanna opened that nightstand drawer and found a Bible, a tablet, several pens, a sharpened pencil, a small dictionary, and a devotional book. Curious, she opened the devotional book to the daily message. It cited the familiar verses from the book of Ruth:

"Don't beg me to leave you or to stop following you. Where you

go, I will go. Where you live, I will live. Your people will be my people, and your God will be my God."

Tanna knew the verses by heart and recited them without looking at the text. She knew they were the words spoken by a widowed daughter-in-law to her widowed mother-in-law, but she had chosen them as her marriage vows. Another character in the book of Ruth had come to life for her when Josh proposed. He packed a picnic lunch, and they hiked into the hills near Cedar Creek. Josh spread out a blanket and unpacked glasses, plates, silverware, and cloth napkins.

"Fancy! That looks like my mom's china and crystal. How did you talk her into letting you use them?"

"I just had to sweet talk her a little and give her the title to my car as collateral." Josh grinned and started unpacking the wicker picnic basket. It looked like he'd brought her favorite quinoa salad, crackers, and lemon water.

Tanna tasted the salad and tilted her head to one side. "Mmmm. This is really good. Who made it?"

"I did." Josh tapped his finger on his chest. At her skeptical expression, he said, "What?"

"When did you learn how to make quinoa salad?"

"I don't know how to make quinoa salad."

Tanna tilted her head. "You said you made this."

"I did. That's pearl barley instead of quinoa. Try the crackers. They're barley too, but I didn't make them."

Tanna took a small bite of the cracker while Josh expectantly watched. "It tastes like a cracker." Tanna raised her eyebrows. "I don't think I've ever had barley crackers before."

Josh reached for the water and poured it into a glass. "Try this."

Tanna tentatively took a sip of the water. "It tastes like lemons but what else is in it?"

"Guess."

Tanna looked at the water in her glass and tasted it again. "I don't know. Vanilla?"

Josh grinned and shook his head. "No."

"Well, whatever it is, it colors the water a little. That's why I thought it might be vanilla, but I have no idea."

"It's barley water with lemon and honey. It's really healthy so drink up."

"What's with all the barley?" Tanna's head tilted to one side.

Josh reached into the picnic basket and pulled out a small box as he knelt on one knee. "I love you, Tanna, and I want to be your Boaz. I know you don't need a Kinsman Redeemer like Ruth did, but if you won't agree to marry me, I'm the one who will need to be rescued." Josh leaned back and waited for Tanna to respond

Looking into Josh's pleading eyes, Tanna smiled. "Yes, I want you to be my Boaz."

CHAPTER SIX

Sunday at Sarah's house was a relaxing day of reading books and playing games after watching an online church service. One of Sarah's neighbors cleared most of the snow from her driveway, leaving a little for Tucker and Jaz to shovel off. The second wave of bad weather had failed to materialize, and the sun was shining.

Josh called after lunch while Tucker and Jaz were outside shoveling and playing in the snow. He sounded very tired but thankful that all the cows and calves were doing well. Tanna encouraged him to take a nap and promised to have the children call him later.

Monday morning dawned clear and sunny with no wind to move the new snow. Tanna had received an email Sunday night that there would be a delayed start to the school day so students and teachers who were temporarily living without electricity wouldn't have to dress and eat breakfast in the dark. Even so, Tanna expected some of her students to decide it was too difficult to come to school at all after a weekend without water and electricity. Tanna didn't really blame them, and she was thankful for the hot shower and breakfast at her mom's home. Taking the short walk to school in the morning by herself before her children had finished their breakfasts was an added bonus, and Sarah had assured her she would make sure Jaz and Tucker were on time but not too early for school.

While walking, Tanna made plans for her shorter-than-usual classes. She didn't want to proceed with her plans for *Romeo and Juliet* without some of her students, so she came up with a creative writing project that her missing students could easily work on at home. She was also thinking about Siobhan and didn't want her to fall even further behind by missing the class discussion and notes.

The school was eerily quiet when Tanna walked in the front door, and she hoped she had reminded her mom to make sure Tucker and Jaz were dressed warmly enough. While she trudged up the steps to her classroom, her thoughts randomly darted from Sarah's advice that God could make her love story right to the tragic events in *Romeo and Juliet*. She wondered what two teenage, star-crossed lovers could teach her.

Listen to Me.

Just like that, she felt the guilt of looking for answers from everyone but God. *I'm sorry, Lord. I didn't mean to leave You out of the equation.*

Three.

Are you reminding me that Josh and I don't have to figure this out on our own, or has my imagination shifted into overdrive again?

Frowning, Tanna stepped onto the third floor and came face to face with Mrs. Majhor.

"Good morning. You're here early. You did get the message about a late start, didn't you?"

"Oh, yes, I just have a few things to do before my students come." Tanna smiled at the dean of students. "That was quite the storm. Do you know if any of the teachers won't be able to make it to school today?"

"None that I'm aware of, but who knows what the morning will bring. I'm surprised you're here. Wasn't your area, west of town, hit pretty hard?"

"Yes, our electricity will be off for a long time, but the kids and I spent most of the weekend with my mom in town. I feel sorry for anyone who doesn't have electricity today." Tanna turned toward her room but hesitated. "Do you know where Siobhan's grandparents live? I wonder if she'll be in school today."

"They live in town, but I haven't heard anything from them since Friday when I called about Siobhan's in-school suspension. I talked to her auntie, and I couldn't tell if she was angry with me or Siobhan. Oh, by the way, apparently Siobhan prefers to be called 'Vonnie' because she doesn't like her name. Her dad named her, and the two were very close until he deserted both Siobhan and her mother for another woman. At least, that's what Auntie told me. The poor girl has a right to be angry."

Tanna nodded her head in agreement. "I don't know anything about her dad, but I remember being in junior high when her mother was in high school. During her senior year, she led the basketball and track teams to state championships, and, if I remember correctly, she was also the homecoming queen. All the girls in my class wanted to be just like her. It's a sad situation all around. Now, we have to figure out how to reach inside the shell Siobhan has built around herself without breaking anything. It won't be easy."

Mrs. Majhor pressed her lips together. "All we can do is try our best, and I know you will. I think I heard that Siobhan's—I guess I should say Vonnie's—parents met in college, but I don't know where Mr. Lynch is from." Mrs. Majhor stopped talking when footsteps were heard coming up the steps, and Tanna knew their conversation should end as Monica emerged.

"I better get to work before my students come." Tanna walked to her classroom, rummaging in her purse for her keys. After unlocking the door, she turned to Monica who was unlocking her door across the hall. "Good morning, Monica. How was your weekend?"

Monica's shoulders slumped, and she dramatically held her hand to her forehead. "It was awful. I had plans to meet my boyfriend in Bismarck, but I knew I couldn't go after it started sleeting. Did I tell you I have a new boyfriend?"

Tanna shook her head. "I don't think so. You'll have to tell me all about him sometime. I'm glad you didn't try to drive in that weather." Tanna walked into her room and turned back with a smile, hoping to discourage Monica from entering. "I have to type and print the directions for a creative writing project I'm using in my English classes. Hopefully, we won't be missing too many students. I'll talk to you later."

Tanna walked away from Monica and took off her coat. As she hung it in the metal cabinet just inside the classroom door, she was relieved to see Monica going into her classroom. The first thing Tanna did was write some lines from *Romeo and Juliet* on the white board.

"What's in a name? That which we call a rose
By any other word would smell as sweet."
Romeo and Juliet (Act II Scene 2)

After typing out the project directions and printing one copy, she walked to the office to make multiple copies for her classes and to fill her coffee cup. She wrote Siobhan's name on one of the pages and took it to the Detention Room, but no one was there, so she left it on the desk with a couple of pieces of composition paper.

She was finishing her coffee when two students walked in the room. "What do we need for class?"

It was a question she heard every day despite repeating the same answer: "Your book, notebook, and a pen or pencil." Today, she had a different answer: "Just a pen."

By the time the bell rang, she noted that most of her first period students were present. Siobhan was in the detention room, and three other students were missing, but that was not unusual for a Monday morning. Some of them could still be coming.

"On Friday, we talked about Romeo expressing his love for Juliet when he sees her on her balcony. She doesn't see or hear him, and now, it's her turn to express her love for Romeo. Since her family and Romeo's family are enemies, she doesn't want him to be a member of the Montague family. Remember, she doesn't know that he can see and hear her when she says what I have written on the board."

Tanna walked over to the board and quoted Shakespeare's words from the second act of *Romeo and Juliet*. "'What's in a name? That which we call a rose by any other word would smell as sweet.'"

After she wrote her name on the board, she told them the meaning and origin of her name. "'Tanna' is a shortened version of my Gigi Tatiana's name. My brother started calling her 'Gigi' because he was too young to say 'Grammy' so I called her that, too. 'Tatiana' means 'fairy queen,' and it's Russian because her parents were Germans who lived in Russia. My first and middle name were both my grandmothers' names. I knew my Gigi Tatiana, but my Grammy Josephine died before I was born. She was my dad's mom. The name 'Josephine' is Hebrew and means 'Jehovah increases.' It's a feminine version of 'Joseph,' and that was my great grandpa's name."

Tanna distributed the list of instructions and continued with her explanation. "I looked up my names which you can also do, and you may also include the meaning of your last name. It's all on this handout I'm giving you. Write a composition about your name explaining what your name means and if you are named after someone. You may also include if you like your name. When I was younger, I didn't appreciate my middle name because I thought it was too old fashioned, but my dad told me many interesting stories about her. She sounded like a cool old lady, and I'm trying to follow in her footsteps. Don't you agree?"

"Du-wal-ay!" Several students uttered the familiar slang word used in place of "whatever" or "as if," but those who said it were smiling.

Before the bell rang, Tanna gave them time to start researching the meaning of their names and reminded them their compositions were due tomorrow.

THE MORNING PASSED QUICKLY, but Tanna's planning period was interrupted by a phone call from Mrs. Majhor asking if Vonnie could spend the period in Tanna's room. The detention room attendant had left for an appointment, and the dean of students had a meeting scheduled in her office. Tanna thought it was nice of her to ask, but she knew she really didn't have a choice.

When Siobhan walked into her room, Tanna noticed that she didn't have any paper or pens with her. "Did you finish reading the first two acts of *Romeo and Juliet?*"

Siobhan shrugged one shoulder, but Tanna was determined to draw her out. "How was your weekend?"

When Siobhan didn't respond, Tanna tried again. "Did your electricity go off? Ours is still off, but my kids and I spent the weekend in town at my Mom's house."

Siobhan finally looked at Tanna with an impatient look. "Mrs. Majhor said I was s'pose ta work in here this period, but I wanna use the bathroom first."

"Okay. Use the one on this floor, and then I'll give you your assignment." Tanna watched Siobhan slowly walk down the hall, looking in every open classroom door as she passed

Lord, give me a little help here, please.

When Siobhan hadn't returned five minutes later, Tanna looked down the hallway and saw the young girl stepping out of the bathroom. Once again, she gazed into each of the open doors and leisurely made her way back to the classroom. Smiling and shaking her head, Tanna walked to the white board to repair parts of a few letters her last-period students had erased as they ran their fingers through them.

When Siobhan finally returned, Tanna handed her a piece of paper and a pen. "You're going to be writing about your name today, so what name do you want me to call you? Mrs. Majhor said you prefer 'Vonnie.' Is that right?"

"Yeah. Whatever. I won't be here that long."

"Do you mean today? Yes, you'll go back to the office after the bell rings, or did Mrs. Majhor tell you to go to another classroom?"

"I won't be in this stupid school that long, so I don't care what you call me. What do I gotta write about?" Vonnie's lowered eyebrows cautioned Tanna it was time to quit trying to draw this troubled girl into a conversation.

Don't give up. Talk to her.

Tanna paused and then sat in the chair across the aisle from Vonnie. "Where did you go to school before coming here?"

"That was a stupid school, too, but at least they let us leave for lunch."

"That would be nice. Where did you eat lunch then?"

Vonnie shrugged one of her shoulders. "Usually at home when we lived closer to the school. After we had ta move, wherever I could get something." Vonnie leaned back in her chair and started drumming her fingers on the desk top.

Tanna felt like she was walking through a minefield. *Help, I'm flying in the dark here.*

"I suppose there were a lot more students and class choices there."

"Yeah, I guess. Are you gonna give me the assignment, or what?" Vonnie extended her hand palm up.

Tanna tried not to stare at the exposed tell-tale, white scars on Vonnie's arm when she reached for the assignment sheet.

"It's due tomorrow," she said. "And should be at least two hundred words long with a title and written in ink. Let me know if you have any questions."

Tanna rose and walked to her desk before Vonnie could see the horror in her eyes. She wanted nothing more than to embrace the girl and tell her everything would be all right, but of course, Tanna couldn't make that promise. The small white scars she saw were definitely from "cutting." Earlier that year, in a teachers' in-service, an expert had said it is a form of self-injury used to cope with or control emotional pain. A former student confided to her that she sliced small cuts in her flesh to release the hurt she was feeling, but the girl also admitted the relief was temporary.

At least Vonnie's cuts didn't appear to be fresh—not on that arm anyway.

The bell rang, and Tanna closed her classroom door, locking it from the inside. It was her lunch break, so she sat at her desk and lowered her head.

Lord, what can I do to help her?

CHAPTER SEVEN

The sunshine filtered through the blinds into Sarah's living room as she sank down onto the leather recliner. When she moved to town, she had left most of her furniture in the ranch house or given it to Matt. Sam had preferred leather and solid oak living and dining room furniture, but she had wanted something lighter and softer for her new home. What she really wanted to do was make everything so different that she wouldn't be able to picture Sam there.

The hardest part of being a widow was accepting that nothing would ever be the same again. Sam had made her feel protected and cherished, and she was lost without him. One of the reasons she couldn't give up Sam's recliner was because she felt that same protection every time she sat in it.

Her weariness didn't come from working too hard. Feeding her grandchildren and walking them to school actually revitalized her after a restless night, but now she needed time to think. Last night, after leaving Tanna, she had looked up familiar Bible verses, hoping to find something definitive to help Tanna with her dilemma, but she had fallen asleep reading her Bible.

Sarah had awakened several times during the night with

an uneasy feeling. The first time, she walked out to check if all the doors were locked and if the stove burners had been turned off. Everything seemed to be in order, and she quickly fell asleep again only to wake with a start an hour later. After walking down the hall to see if one of the children had cried out, she found them sleeping soundly. Shivering, she returned to her bedroom and prayed that God would help her advise Tanna.

After tossing and turning for half an hour, she walked to the living room and settled into the overstuffed loveseat. "All right, Lord, I'm listening."

Letting her mind wander, Sarah's thoughts drifted from Matt as a baby to her mother and back to a trip she and Sam had taken to Mount Rushmore with Matt and Tanna when they were children. The peaceful, contented feeling caused her to relax and hover between sleep and awareness until she woke feeling confused and sad. There was also a feeling of deep melancholy. She knew she had been dreaming, but as hard as she tried, she couldn't recall the details.

Throughout the day, Sarah carried around the same anxious feeling, and she finally sank to her knees and prayed. Worried that someone in her family was the cause of her uneasiness, she started with Matt and named each of her children, their spouses, and her grandchildren. She expressed her love and thankfulness for them and asked the Lord to protect them. Sarah distractedly caught herself praying for Sam. It felt so good to forget, even just for a moment, that he was gone.

"Why did You let him die, Lord? He was a good man and so faithful to You."

I AM WHO I AM.

Confused, Sarah's eyebrows drew together. The words

from Exodus were familiar, but what did they mean for her now?

Sam.

"What does Sam…" Before she could finish her question, she knew the answer. It was time to give Sam to the Lord. She would see him again, but she didn't want to wish for a speedy end to her life so she could be with him in heaven. For over forty years, Sam had been willing to make important decisions in their lives and have the difficult conversations she avoided. He would have known how to counsel Tanna about her marriage.

After Sam died, she had struggled to perform even the easiest tasks. She had no idea when her car needed an oil change or new tires. He had always taken care of all their major finances and purchases, while Sarah had paid the household bills and kept their checkbook balanced. It was just so much easier to let Sam take care of the insurance and taxes, and he had readily obliged. She hadn't even known where their records were stored, and she'd been angry that Sam had left her without a plan. Even her prayers were not the same without her husband kneeling beside her or holding her hand as they prayed. He had been her rock, and she was lost without him. With Sam, she had everything she needed and wanted.

"Lord, why didn't You give me and Sam some warning?"

———

THE FINAL BELL rang and Tanna walked to the office, hoping Mrs. Majhor's expertise could help her deal with Vonnie's problems. A heavy feeling had shadowed her all day, and she just needed to talk to someone.

"How did Vonnie do today?" Tanna asked.

"She spent a lot of time looking out the window, but we really didn't have any problems with her. How was she when she came to your room?"

"She said she doesn't plan to be here very long. Is that true?"

"Her auntie said they don't know where her mom is, so I don't know where she would go."

"What about her dad. Could she be thinking of going wherever he is? It sounds like she liked living in Sioux Falls."

"I don't think that's an option. It sounds like he pretty much cut all ties to Vonnie and her mom. I asked her if I could read the composition you assigned. I wanted to see if she completed the assignment, but I also wanted to see if she is close to writing on her grade level." Mrs. Majhor handed Vonnie's paper to Tanna.

"And what did you decide?'

"Her skills are somewhat lacking."

Tanna glanced at Vonnie's paper. "She certainly has artistic handwriting. How well does she express herself?" Tanna looked up from the paper to Mrs. Majhor.

"Actually, very well, but maybe I think that because I could hear the pain when she talked about her name. She doesn't like it because it was her dad who came up with the name 'Siobhan.' She said he thought it went perfectly with their Lynch last name. It sounds like he was determined to make her Irish like his family, but then he deserted both Siobhan and her mother for another woman. Now, her mom has basically deserted her, too."

"I noticed something else when she was in my room that we'll have to monitor, although, I don't know what we can do about it. She has cutting marks on her arm. What I saw

My Portion Forever

didn't look fresh, but I don't know if there were hidden, fresh cuts."

The office phone rang, and Tanna left with a wave as Mrs. Majhor answered it.

Tanna read Vonnie's paper while she walked, but as she approached her classroom, she heard Jaz and Tucker calling to her as they ran to meet her.

"Can we walk to Grammy's house, or do we have to wait for you?"

"Just a minute. Let me call Grammy to make sure she's home."

After a brief conversation with Sarah, Tanna told her children they could wait inside the main doors of the school for their grandma to pick them up. "Remember that Jaz in in charge until Grammy comes, so you have to listen to her, Tucker. Do you understand?" Tanna made them look at her and agree with her directions. "Jaz and Tucker, be a blessing while you are with Grammy. Okay?"

She waited for both of them to say, "Okay, Mommy." She watched out her door as they walked down the hall to the steps, and then she returned to her desk to read Vonnie's composition.

A Pretty Name for a Pretty Girl?

My name is Siobhan Rose Lynch and I wasn't named after anybody I know except the Lynch part. That's my dad's last name. I know it's Irish because he always talked about how wonderful it is to be Irish. He picked my name Siobhan Rose because he thought it sounded good with Lynch. He told me it was a pretty name for a pretty girl. When I was little, I believed everything he told me. Now I don't know if any of its true. I don't like my name because nobody can say it or spell it. Your the only teacher who says it right and talks to me about stuff. Some of the dumb kids in my Sioux Falls school called me Sioux Bee even when my teachers told them not to. The friends I had their called me Vonnie but after my dad left and me and my mom had to move to a dumpy apartment they quit hanging out with me. I looked up my name and found out it has Hebrew origins and the meaning of Siobhan is God is gracious. Thats kind of cool I guess if you believe in that kinda stuff.

The End

Tanna read the composition twice and agreed with the dean of students. She could hear the pain in Vonnie's essay, but the phrase that kept drawing her back to Vonnie's words were the last ones: "The meaning of Siobhan is God is gracious. That's kind of cool I guess if you believe in that kind of stuff."

Apparently, Vonnie didn't believe in "that kind of stuff," but maybe Tanna could talk to her if—and that was a big "if"—she had another opportunity to meet privately with her troubled student.

Tanna sat back in her chair and enjoyed the luxury of knowing her children were being cared for while she worked.

―――

SARAH WAS SEARCHING her Bible for some passages that would soothe her troubled thoughts when Tanna called about the children coming to her house. The day had passed quickly, and Sarah checked the clock doubtful that school could be over already. Before she pulled on her boots, coat, gloves, and hat, she stopped at her freezer to take out some cookies.

As she exited her garage, Sarah saw children already walking by on their way home. Glancing at her watch, she picked up her pace on the short walk to the back doors of the school. Jaz and Tucker burst out of the glass doors just as she approached the building. They were ready to run the two blocks to her house, but she warned them there wouldn't be cookies for anyone who didn't wait for her.

"Grammy, what kind of cookies do you have?" Tucker's eyes twinkled as he smiled at Sarah.

"The best kind."

"What kind is that?" Jaz took Sarah's hand and waited for an answer.

Sarah stopped walking and looked at her grandchildren with her mouth open. "Why, the ones made with love, of course."

"But what *kind* did you make with love?" Jaz pulled on Sarah's hand, wordlessly urging her to keep walking.

"I'll tell you after you hang up your coats and wash your hands, okay? And don't forget to take your boots off in the garage."

"We will, Grammy." Tucker let go of her hand to open the garage door. He waited for Sarah and Jaz to go in before he entered and pushed it shut.

"Thank you, Tucker. That was very polite of you."

"Daddy says men should always let ladies go in first."

Jaz took off her boots and laughed as she opened the door into Sarah's house. "You're not a man, Tucker. You're a boy."

"Boys are men aren't they, Grammy?"

Sarah nodded her head as she followed Tucker into the house. "Yes, Tucker, boys are little men."

Tucker lifted his chin and scrunched up his mouth and nose at Jaz as he passed her. Before Jaz could continue the dispute, Sarah interrupted, "Wash your hands, and remember, quarrelling children can't have cookies that are made with love."

Sarah and the children were still sitting at the table when Tanna came home from school. She picked up a napkin and wiped away Tucker's milk mustache before he squirmed away and grabbed the last cookie.

"Didn't you save some cookies for me?"

Tucker froze, the cookie inches from his open mouth, and sheepishly offered the cookie to her.

"No, you can keep it, but how many have you had?"

Sarah picked up the glasses and napkins. "I gave them each two cookies. Is that too many?"

"No!" Jaz and Tucker said in unison.

Tanna smiled and shook her head. "Let's make some rules about snacking after school. When Matt and I were in school, Grammy told us we had to have healthy snacks after school at least three times a week. At home, you always have fruit or granola bars."

"But that's because you never make cookies, Mommy. These are special circumstances." Tucker beamed and Tanna reached over to ruffle his hair as she rose from her chair.

"Let's call Daddy and see how everything is at home."

CHAPTER EIGHT

Josh reluctantly hung up the phone after talking to his family for almost an hour. They had both laughed when Tucker excitedly told him about the boys versus the girls in a preschool-snowman-building contest during the lunch recess.

"Then before we had to go inside, the girls got to knock down the boys' snowman, and the boys made the girls' snowman, flat." Josh heard Tucker clap his hands once and giggle. When Josh asked him who won, Tucker told him, "We all did! And, Daddy, I held the door open for Grammy and Jaz after school because you told me that's what men do."

"I'm proud of you for being polite and helpful, Son, and I want you to keep on looking out for Jaz and Mom. Will you do that for me?"

"Sure. Grammy, too? She walks around in the house all night, so I think she thinks that's her job."

Josh laughed. "Sometimes, Grammys just like to do that, but you can watch out for her, too."

Tucker wondered how the cows and calves were doing and was happy to hear they were all safe. Finally, Tucker wanted to know if he could come home soon, but his dad couldn't give him an answer. "Sorry, Buddy. I miss you guys, too."

Jaz read to him from the library book she had brought home from school and asked if he was taking care of the cats in the barn. He told her the cats were snug and warm and asked her if she was being helpful around Grammy's house.

"Yes, Daddy, I set the table and make my bed, but that's not easy on the top bunk." She didn't ask about coming home, but Josh knew she missed him when she asked him if he would call her back to say good night before she went to bed.

By the time he spoke to Tanna, she was distracted by the children saying they were hungry and ready to eat. Eventually, Josh heard Sarah telling them to come with her into the kitchen so Tanna and Josh could have a little time to themselves.

"It's too quiet around here, and I really miss your cooking... Oh, shoot! I have this burner turned up too high. I'm making scrambled eggs for supper, and I don't know how you make them so fluffy." Josh waited for Tanna's response and thought he heard her sniffle. "Are you all right?"

After another sniff, Tanna sighed, "It's probably too late if you're already frying them. I'll let you go so you can finish. Sounds like that's all you can concentrate on now. Bye." She hung up before he could respond.

Josh stared at the phone as if he expected it to tell him why Tanna had hung up so abruptly, but he shifted his attention back to rescuing his eggs before they burned. He would ask her if she was okay when he called later before Jaz and Tucker went to bed.

He missed having her here and not just because she was a better cook. After they left to stay in town with Sarah, he had been busy taking care of the cattle and keeping the house warm without electricity, but now that he'd settled into a routine, he felt at loose ends most of the day. He wanted to see her when he came into the house and when he crawled into their cold bed at night. He missed talking to her about their day after Jaz and Tucker went to bed. Without her, there was no joy in their home, and it occurred to him that it didn't feel like a home when she was absent.

The scent of the house was even different when she was gone. He closed his eyes and imagined walking into the house when Tanna was there. The first fragrance that came to mind was vanilla, but that was quickly replaced with her perfume. He couldn't describe it except that it was fresh and reminded him of his beautiful and adventurous wife. *When was the last time I told her how beautiful I think she is?*

Before moving to the ranch, Tanna had always hugged him when he came home from work, and he had often told her he didn't know what he had ever done to deserve the best and prettiest wife. When had that stopped?

He shook his head and went through the motions of eating, but his turbulent memories filled his mind, and he didn't notice how his eggs tasted. As he cleaned up the dishes afterward, he tried to think of a way to make things right with their marriage, but that involved revealing what Sam had told him. How could he do that without spoiling her image of her parents' marriage? She had always held it up as the gold standard of marriages, but it was time to tell her the truth.

TANNA WAS quiet and withdrawn after her phone conversation with Josh, and Sarah was unable to draw her out of the gloomy web that surrounded her. Tucker and Jaz kept up a lively conversation while they ate their supper of cheese buttons and sausage. Sam had liked to have sauerkraut with this German dish, but neither Tanna nor her children were fans, so Sarah eliminated that from the menu. Instead, she served raw carrots and celery.

She smiled when she told Tucker and Jaz "Papa called this rabbit food."

Her grandchildren loved to hear stories about Sam, and she loved to tell them.

She had learned how to make this traditional German dish from her mother, who made her own dry curd cottage cheese to fill the noodle pouches that became the "buttons." Now that Sam wasn't there to notice the difference, Sarah sometimes cheated and used ricotta cheese.

Tucker seemed to notice his mom's withdrawn demeanor but quit trying to talk to her after challenging Jaz to a cheese-button-eating contest. Tanna snapped out of her sullenness when he stuffed two in his mouth. She told him he'd had enough and to finish his vegetables.

"Thanks for supper, Mom. I think I'll soak in your tub after I clean up the kitchen if you don't mind putting the kids to bed and letting them use your bathroom. Josh told Jaz he'd call before she went to bed, and Tucker will probably want to talk to him again, too. Remind them not to talk too long. They use any excuse not to go to bed, and they already talked to Josh once today."

When the phone rang, Jaz asked if she could answer it. Her delighted chatter indicated that it was Josh calling to say "good night." Tanna told Sarah she was off to take her bath

My Portion Forever

and reminded Tucker that he should wait until Jaz was through talking. Sarah started to ask Tanna if she wanted to talk to Josh but swallowed her words as her daughter abruptly walked to the bathroom, where she stayed until her mom and children were in their bedrooms.

Sarah wanted to talk to Tanna, but she hesitated when she heard her leave the bathroom and walk down the hall. Surely Tanna could see that her mom's bedroom light was on if she wanted to talk.

Lord, how can I help my daughter?

She believed Tanna had made the right choice when she chose Josh to marry, but her opinion didn't really matter. She knew how headstrong her daughter was, so she hadn't been surprised when her advice to Tanna to take her time had seemed to fall on deaf ears. Her daughter had made a decision within a few days and then proceeded to rush full steam ahead. It hurt her heart to see her only daughter struggling, but she didn't know what to do about it.

Ask Me.

There it was again. Another random thought that popped into her head.

"Is that You, Lord, or am I imagining it? I have asked You, but You don't answer me, just like You won't tell me why Sam had to die. I'm sorry if I sound angry, but Sam would know how to handle this situation with Tanna and Josh. More than likely, he would tell me not to worry. Will You at least tell me that? If only…"

Sarah drifted off to sleep, waiting to hear some words of wisdom, but a searing pain woke her abruptly several hours later. She left her bed to walk toward the door, holding her hand on the side of her face. The pain traveled along her jaw from her ear toward her mouth and was so intense she couldn't think clearly. Within a minute, the pain ended as suddenly as it had begun, and Sarah crawled back into bed.

Once the horrible pain was gone, it seemed like a bad dream, but it was like no other nightmare she had ever had. It reminded her of a similar pain she had felt several months ago when she was in the shower. She had brushed a washcloth across her brow and felt the same searing pain except it had traveled across her forehead. It seemed to happen only when she showered, but not every time. She had just assumed it was a sinus infection. It didn't bother her any other time, but it worried her that now she felt the electrical-like shooting pain in a different part of her face. She drifted back into a troubled sleep, determined to call the clinic in the morning.

CHAPTER NINE

Another school day ended, and Tanna sat quietly in her classroom with her eyes closed, waiting for an answer. Earlier she had gone to the Alternative Room to deliver assignments to Vonnie. She was the only student in the room, and the monitor had asked Tanna if she minded staying while he took a break. Tanna welcomed the opportunity to connect with Vonnie, but that hope died when the girl's indifferent responses silenced Tanna's attempts at conversation. After the monitor returned, Tanna had slowly walked to her classroom, feeling defeated. *What can I do, Lord? She needs You so badly, but I can't reach her no matter how hard I try. What am I doing wrong?*

The phone rang, startling Tanna, and it took a moment to regain an awareness of her surroundings. "Hello?"

"Tanna, can you come down to the elementary office? The principal would like to talk to you."

Tanna tried to steady her voice. "Has something happened to Jaz or Tucker?"

"Oh, no. It's about Jaz, but it's nothing to worry about."

"Okay. I'll be right down." Tanna gathered her purse and keys and walked to the door as the custodian entered with his dust mop.

"Leaving early today? Do you want me to lock your door after I finish?" The custodian picked up the garbage basket to empty it.

"Yes, I don't plan to come back today, and if I do, I have my key. Thanks. See you tomorrow." Tanna stepped out of her room with a wave.

Jaz was waiting outside the principal's office and ran to Tanna when she saw her approaching. "Mom, hurry up. Mr. Jackson is waiting for you."

Tanna looked into the principal's office. "Where is Tucker? Did he stay in the library with Mrs. Philips?"

"Uh, no. Tucker went up to your room. Didn't you see him?"

The principal called out to Jaz and Tanna that they could come in, but Tanna looked at Jaz with a worried expression. "Maybe, you could find Tucker and bring him down here while I talk to Mr. Jackson."

"But I wanna be there when Mr. Jackson talks to you, Mom!"

Tanna chewed her lip. "Maybe I can call up to my room. If Jack is still sweeping, he can send him down."

Betty, the elementary secretary, rolled her chair away from her desk and stood. "I'll go up to look for him. You two go on into the office." She pointed to Mr. Jackson's door. "Don't worry. I'll bring him back here. Now, go!"

Mr. Jackson thanked Tanna for coming and closed his office door. As he rearranged the folders on his desk, Tanna began to doubt that he was preparing to give her good news, but he finally sat down and winked at Jaz before he directed his attention to Tanna.

"We have a good little reader here, and we want to put her into a second-grade reading group. What do you think about that?" He folded his hands on his desk and looked from Jaz to Tanna.

"Yes! Please, Mom. I'd be in the same group as Melissa."

Tanna looked questioningly at the principal, and he nodded his agreement. "Yes, one of the girls in her class is already in that group."

"It sounds like a good idea to me if her teacher agrees." Tanna brushed the hair out of Jaz's eyes and turned back to the principal.

"She suggested it, but she had to leave early today for an appointment. Would you rather talk to her about this?"

"No. If she recommended it, I trust her judgment. Okay, let's do it then." Tanna put her arm around Jaz and smiled. "Now we better go find your brother."

When Tanna and Jaz walked out of the principal's office, no one was at the secretary's desk.

"Tucker must still be up in my room, Jaz. Do you want to wait here or go with me to find him?"

"I'll go with you. I bet he's making a pest of himself in your room."

"I wonder who taught him to be a pest?" Tanna nudged Jaz and raised an eyebrow.

Jaz and Tanna walked down the hallway laughing but stopped when they saw the secretary approaching, alone.

Tanna quickened her pace until she met Betty, but Betty held up her hands. "Don't worry. He's in your room working on his Bible memory verse with a high school girl, and Jack said he'd keep an eye on your room."

"A high school girl?"

"Yes, I don't know her name, but Tucker seemed to know her."

Tanna thanked the elementary secretary and briskly

walked to the stairway. Jaz ran to keep up and sensed that her mom was upset about something.

Tanna caught her breath as she entered her classroom. Tucker was standing by her desk, facing a smiling and nodding Vonnie, who jumped up from the desk chair when Tanna approached. "I'm sorry. Tucker told me it was all right to sit here. I didn't touch nothing."

"That's fine, Vonnie. Do you need something?"

"I wanted to know if I could have those notes from the first act of *Romeo and Juliet*." Vonnie nervously fingered the buttons on her jacket. "I read it today, and I liked it."

"Sure. Let me find them."

While Tanna unlocked her file cabinet, Tucker tapped Vonnie's arm. "Don't forget what I told you."

A smile lit up Vonnie's face. "You got it."

Tanna handed Vonnie a folder. "Here are the notes, and there is also a writing assignment that you missed. It's not due until Friday, and I'll give you my cell number in case you have questions. I turn off my phone at 11:00, so you'll have to call before then." Tanna jotted the number on the folder and smiled, hoping to get the same response, but Vonnie took the folder without looking at her before she left the room.

"Who was that girl, Mom?" Tanna didn't respond or even seem to hear Jaz's question, so Jaz touched her mom's hand and asked again.

"Her name is Siobhan. She's a freshman." Tanna answered Jaz without taking her eyes off of Tucker.

Tucker shook his head. "Nuh-uh. Her name is Vonnie. She's my friend."

Jaz scowled at Tucker. "She's too old to be your friend. You're only four, and she's in high school." She looked at

Tanna hopefully. "She's so pretty. I can't wait until I can pierce my ears like hers."

"We'll talk about it in about ten years, Honey."

Jaz's shoulders slumped, and Tanna turned her attention back to Tucker. "Her name is Siobhan, but she likes to be called Vonnie. What were you two talking about?"

"When?" Tucker scrunched up his face.

Tanna sighed and put her arm around him. "Let's start with what you told her not to forget."

"Well." Tucker gestured with one hand. "First, I asked her if she would listen to my Bible verse for Sunday school, and she said 'sure.' Then she said she wouldn't know if it was right or not, but I told her not to worry because I was pretty sure I knew it by heart. After I said it, she told me I did a good job."

Jaz and Tanna both listened to Tucker tell his story, complete with hand gestures and facial expressions, but Jaz seemed doubtful. "What is your memory verse?"

"'God loved the world so much that he gave his one and only Son so that whoever believes in him may not be lost, but have eternal life.' John 3:16." Tucker looked at his mom for approval.

Tanna clapped her hands. "That's perfect, Tucker."

"Then, Vonnie asked me what 'eternal life' is so I told her it's heaven and that's where you go when you die if you have Jesus in your heart. Right, Mommy?"

"Absolutely, Tucker. Good job." Tanna smiled at her son. "I have two very smart children." Tanna hugged both of them.

"What did you tell her not to forget?" Jaz was still feeling a little doubtful.

"I told her she could memorize that verse, but she said

she didn't have a Bible, so I told her she could find it on the computer. All she had to remember is John 3:16. But...but... you could give her a Bible. Couldn't you, Mommy?" Tucker looked hopefully at Tanna.

Tanna pointed to Tucker. "I think you should give her a Bible the next time you see her. We'll have to see what we can find at Grammy's house. Now, let's go home and tell Grammy all our good news."

Tanna's heart soared as she walked out of the school with her children.

"Grammy, I'm here!" Tucker looked around the kitchen as he raced ahead of Jaz and Tanna. A Tupperware container sat on the counter, and Tucker pulled the note off of it. He waved it in Tanna's face. "Grammy left a note, I think. What does it say?"

"It says to have a cookie. She'll be home later." Tanna read the note and then turned it over, looking for more of an explanation. "I guess she had something to do. Tucker, will you give us each a napkin? Jaz, I'll take the milk out of the refrigerator if you find us some glasses. Let's celebrate."

They were finishing their milk and cookies when they heard Sarah's car pull into the garage. Tanna hadn't noticed that her mom's car was gone when they had walked into the breezeway beside the garage. She had just assumed Sarah had walked to one of her neighbor's houses or down the block to the post office.

"Grammy! Guess what?" Tucker jumped up and down in front of Sarah as she entered the kitchen.

"You built the biggest snowman at recess today." Sarah lifted an eyebrow.

"No! It's better than that. Jaz and I both have big news."

"Let me tell Grammy first." Jaz looked hopefully from Tucker to Tanna for approval.

Tanna looked at Tucker. "I think that's a good idea. Don't you?"

Tucker folded his arms and nodded his head. "Ladies first."

CHAPTER TEN

Sarah's phone rang as they finished supper, and both children raced to the telephone.

"It's my turn, Jaz. You answered it last night." Tucker blocked the way as Jaz tried to push passed him. "Mom, it's my turn."

"Grammy is going to answer it before whoever is calling hangs up." Tanna gestured to her children to move while Sarah squeezed by them.

"Hello, Millie! Hang on just a minute." Sarah covered the phone and pointed down the hall. "It's for me. Tanna, I'm going to take the phone into my bedroom."

"Mommy, can I call Daddy on your cell phone? I want to tell him that I get to be in Second Grade for reading."

"I want to call Daddy, too, and tell him about my new friend."

"She's not your friend." Jaz put her hands on her hips and frowned at Tucker.

After thinking for a moment, Tanna handed her phone to Jaz and helped her make the call. Before Tucker could start complaining, she told him they would look for a Bible to give Vonnie while Jaz was talking on the phone.

Sarah had several bookcases in her home, so Tanna searched the higher shelves as Tucker looked on the lower ones. Tanna noticed that her mother had several books on the loss of a loved one and was again reminded that her mom was still grieving.

Jaz was still talking to Josh when Sarah returned to the living room, and Tucker asked her if she had a Bible he could give to Vonnie.

"I think I have a small New Testament here somewhere. Remember, Tanna, when you and Matt were in school, and some Gideons handed them out after school? They did that several times, and I kept the ones you brought home. I was hoping I could give them to someone."

She handed Tucker a small red book as Jaz approached the group and handed the cell phone to Tanna. "Daddy wants to talk to you."

Reluctantly, Tanna took the phone from Jaz. "Hello."

"Do you think you could come to the ranch this weekend…alone?" Tanna closed her eyes when she recognized the hopeful tone in Josh's voice. After furtively glancing at her children, she left the room.

———

TANNA'S EXPRESSION didn't escape Sarah's notice, so she did what she could to distract the children. "Tucker, maybe we could mark some verses in this little New Testament for your friend."

"She's *not* his friend!" Jaz sniffed and held her hands up in frustration.

"Is *too!*" Tucker faced Jaz with his hands on his hips.

Sarah stepped between her grandchildren and touched their backs, encouraging them to move to the couch where she sat between them. "Jaz, do you know how to find verses in the Bible?"

"A little."

"Then find John thirteen verse thirty-five."

A worried look crossed Jaz's face, but she squinted at the small print as she leafed through the pages. Tucker opened his mouth, but Sarah held up her hand and positioned her index finger over her lips. "Listen! Jaz can you read it?"

Jaz displayed the page to Sarah. "Is this right?" Sarah leaned closer and nodded, and Jaz began to slowly sound out the words, "All…people will…know…that…you are my… followers if you love…each other." She stopped and looked anxiously at Sarah.

"Very good, Jaz. Do you think Jesus wants Tucker to love Vonnie?" Sarah waited for Jaz to nod her head before continuing. "Are you a follower of Jesus?" Jaz nodded again. "Then, Jesus wants you to love Vonnie and Tucker, doesn't He?"

"Yes!" Tucker couldn't contain his excitement. "Grammy, my memory verse says that God loves the world. Vonnie is part of the world. I think."

"Tucker," Jaz frowned, "That still doesn't make her your friend."

"If Jesus is her friend, so am I." Tucker defiantly faced Jaz.

"Let's just agree that Jesus loves all of us and wants us all to be friends. Okay?" Sarah smiled at her grandchildren.

Tucker gave Jaz a lopsided grin. "You can be her friend, too, if you want to. She's really nice. Tomorrow, we could both give her this Bible."

"Hey, what's going on in here? Why all the smiles?" Tanna walked into the room holding her cell phone.

"Jaz is gonna be Vonnie's friend, too. Grammy says that's what Jesus wants."

Tanna looked from Tucker to her mom for an explanation, but then she handed her phone to Tucker. "Tell Daddy all about it."

Tucker ran off with the phone, and Jaz explained that she and Tucker were both going to give the Bible to Vonnie. "Can we do it tomorrow? After school?"

"We'll have to see, Jaz. Vonnie doesn't always come to my room after school."

"But you could tell her to." Jaz raised her eyebrows.

"Yes, I could. We'll see. Now, why don't you brush your teeth and get ready for bed. I'll send Tucker in when he finishes talking to Daddy."

After Jaz left the room, Tanna asked Sarah if she could stay for a while. "I want to talk to you, unless you're too tired."

"I'm fine, and I want to talk to you about something, too."

Sarah brewed a pot of herbal tea while Tanna tucked the children in and had just sat down when Tanna returned to the living room. "How is Josh getting along? Is there any word yet on how much longer the electricity will be off?"

Tanna curled up on the couch with an afghan and reached for the cup of tea Sarah held out to her. "Oh, he's getting along, but he's tired of melting snow. It wouldn't be so bad if all he had to do was melt it, but the snow isn't really clean, even when it looks as white as can be. There's probably a lesson in there somewhere, but I'm too tired to think about it now."

Tanna sipped her tea. "This is good, Mom. Thanks. Anyway, since the snow is much dirtier than it looks, he said he has to strain it and then boil it if he wants to drink it or cook with it. I'll have to remember that the next time Jaz and Tucker want me to eat snow. Did you know it's that dirty? Yuck." Tanna made a face and Sarah laughed at her.

"It didn't hurt you and Matt. You ate your share of snow while you were growing up. It probably made your immune system stronger."

Tanna leaned back and wrapped her hands around the warm cup. "Josh said the linemen came out today and replaced the broken electrical pole. He talked to them before they left, and they didn't know how much longer the electricity would be off. Josh thought now that he can get out of the driveway, he might come to town for groceries and to visit us on Friday." Tanna finished her tea and set her cup down.

Before Sarah could respond, Tanna continued. "There's more. He wants me to go home with him for the weekend—without the kids." Tanna paused, and Sarah waited, not wanting to put a damper on her daughter's obvious excitement before hearing the whole plan. "He said we need to talk. Alone. Mom, he sounded like the old Josh. He almost begged me to come home. He said he'll make a roaring fire in the fireplace, and we can talk until we fall asleep in the living room by the fire." Tanna paused in her narrative, and a flush crept up her face.

Sarah rushed to fill the awkward silence. "That sounds wonderful, honey, and I don't want to spoil things for you, but what will you tell Tucker and Jaz? You know how much they miss Josh and the ranch."

"That's where you come in. If you're willing, I thought maybe you could take them to Pete and Millie's house—just for Friday night and Saturday. You know how Pete and

My Portion Forever

Millie love the kids, and Pete could take them for snowmobile rides. They won't even notice that I'm gone."

"I would love to do that, but aren't you planning to tell Jaz and Tucker where you're going?" Sarah's eyes widened as she gave Tanna a long look. "Why not let them go home for a little while. Maybe Saturday night?"

Tanna's excitement was fading. "I'm afraid if they know where I'm going, they'll be so disappointed that it will ruin the whole weekend for us. Would it be so bad to hide it from them? I could leave on Friday night after they're in bed, and they'll be so excited Saturday morning about snowmobiling that they won't care. If they put up a fuss, you can bring them to the ranch on Saturday night. Mom, this is what I've been hoping and praying for. Josh is ready to talk about us, and I don't want to ruin that…" Tanna's voice trailed off, and her eyes glistened as she looked helplessly at Sarah.

"Let's pray about it. That's what your dad always said in situations like this. If this is an answer to your prayers about Josh, God has a plan. He just needs to show you what it is."

Sarah walked to the couch and sat beside her daughter. Grasping Tanna's hand, Sarah thanked God for loving them and caring about every detail of their lives. She tearfully expressed the urgent need to recognize the leading of the Holy Spirit in their circumstances. When Sarah paused, Tanna added her own pleadings for wisdom to do the right thing, and ended with her own expressions of thanks for God's answers.

"I have to go to bed, or I'll fall asleep in school tomorrow." Tanna yawned and stretched.

"Everything looks better after a good night's sleep. I'll get the light. Just go to bed." Sarah waited until Tanna closed her bedroom door before closing her eyes and spending a little more time praying. She was grateful that Jaz and Tucker's animated stories of their day had helped her forget about the question hanging over her own head. The physician's assistant at the local clinic had run some tests and suggested she go to the dentist, but there had been no answers today to explain her sudden and sharp facial pain.

CHAPTER ELEVEN

When Tanna entered the kitchen to make coffee the next morning, she was surprised to find Sarah sitting at the table, writing a note.

"Mom, you're up early, and you look like you're dressed to go somewhere special." Tanna waited for her mom to explain what she had planned for the day.

"Pete and Millie are on their way over here to pick me up and take me to Bismarck. They should be here any minute. I was just writing you a note explaining everything. I'm sorry we don't have time to talk about your plans for going with Josh to the ranch. Maybe we'll have time tonight."

Tanna wrinkled her brow. "When did you plan this? Is that what you wanted to talk to me about last night?"

Sarah walked to the counter and poured a cup of coffee. She handed it to Tanna as she paused at the table to look out the window. "There they are now. I explained it all in the note. Don't forget to lock the doors before you leave for school. The spare key is hanging by the door. I'll let you know when we leave Bismarck this afternoon. Bye." Sarah buttoned her coat and pulled on her gloves before she opened the door.

Tanna watched her mom walk across the driveway and

climb into Pete's SUV as he held the door open. After they drove away, she lifted the note from the middle of the table.

> Tanna,
> Sorry I didn't have a chance to tell you this last night. Pete and Millie are taking me to the dentist in Bismarck today, and we may not be back until this evening. I'll call you when we leave Bismarck. I took a casserole out of the freezer and put it in the refrigerator for you. Eat as much as you want. We'll probably have something to eat before we leave.
> Love,
> Mom

Tanna shook her head and looked at the door again. Sarah hadn't said anything about going to the dentist last night. An uneasy feeling blanketed Tanna, but the clock told her it was time to shower and wake up Jaz and Tucker.

She set bowls, spoons, and glasses on the table before she left the room to wake her children. They dressed while she showered, and then she told them what she knew about Sarah's absence.

Jaz and Tucker were anxious to see if Vonnie was in the school building, so they ran ahead of her on their way to school. Tanna tried to convince them that she doubted Vonnie would be there that early, but they couldn't contain their excitement. Their enthusiasm was contagious, and Tanna also quickened her pace.

Several students stood by the back door waiting to enter

when Tanna unlocked it, but only a few high school students were in the front lobby. Tucker rushed in and checked all the nooks and crannies and then returned to Tanna and Jaz. "She's not here."

"I'll ask Vonnie to come to my room after school. Okay?" Tanna looked into her children's disappointed faces.

"But we always go to the library." Jaz's lower lip protruded and Tucker's shoulders slumped.

"You can come to my room if you wait until the high school students leave. Your classes are dismissed earlier, remember? I don't want you to burst in while my last class is in session. Just wait outside my door until they leave."

Tanna waited for Jaz and Tucker to each say, "Okay, Mommy."

After walking them to their classrooms, Tanna looked in the usual places the high schoolers liked to hang out after school, but she didn't see Vonnie anywhere. She knew if there were students within earshot when she asked Vonnie to come to her room after school, they would complicate the situation by teasing that Vonnie was either "in trouble" or "the teacher's pet." Vonnie's response in that case would not be pleasant, and she wanted to avoid it if possible. It always amazed her how a student's demeanor often changed when it was just the two of them talking privately.

She finally gave up the search and walked up the stairs to her room. Maybe she could watch for Vonnie in the hallway before her first class started. Tanna put her coat and bag in the metal closet after checking to make sure the red New Testament was still in her bag, and she stood outside her door as more students put their coats into their lockers.

"Are you looking for someone?" Monica exited her room to stand by Tanna.

Before responding, Tanna weighed the situation and decided she could reveal general information. "I'm looking for Vonnie. Have you seen her this morning?"

"No…but…" Monica leaned a little closer and looked around before she whispered, "I was in the office earlier, and her auntie called and said there was a family situation, so she won't be in school today."

Tanna shoulders sagged, and she walked into her room before Monica could proceed with her tale, but Monica followed her. "It sounds like there is a problem with her cousin. You remember him… Trevor?"

"Not really. I wasn't ever his teacher, but I remember hearing his name. He was in elementary school when I taught here before Josh and I married and moved away."

"Well, he's been in treatment for drug abuse, but he's home now. Vonnie's grandparents said he could stay with them until he decides what he wants to do. Auntie wants him to go to college, but he wasn't a very good student, so who knows what he'll end up doing." Monica flashed a wry smile and turned to go as the bell rang.

The morning passed quickly, and Tanna was satisfied with the progress her English classes were making. They seemed genuinely interested in *Romeo and Juliet*, but she couldn't stop thinking about Vonnie and her situation at home. During her planning period, she walked to Mrs. Majhor's office.

"Do you have a minute?" Tanna closed the door before she sat down.

"You've heard about Vonnie's cousin." The dean of students raised her eyebrows and leaned back in her chair.

"Well. Yes. I don't know how much you can tell me, but I am concerned about Vonnie and how it's affecting her."

"There isn't much to tell. Her cousin is back from drug rehab. The family is happy, of course, that he's home, but they are still adjusting to having Vonnie there. I guess all of us will just have to deal with the situation as it develops. I'm concerned about Vonnie, too. She seemed much less defensive when I talked to her after school yesterday. I hope that will continue."

MILLIE HAD INSISTED that Pete stop before they left Cedar Creek so she could move to the back seat to catch up with Sarah. "Pete, you can be the chauffeur, and we'll be the navigators."

"I don't need navigators. I know how to get to Bismarck. You ladies just get all your gabbin' done while I'm drivin' on these country roads. I'll have to concentrate on where I'm goin' after we get to Bismarck." Pete had pointedly looked at Millie. "And don't start yellin' directions at me. I'll ask if I don't know where to go. Now, what's the address for your dentist's office, Sarah?"

After explaining to Pete where she wanted to go, Sarah and Millie didn't stop talking and laughing until they approached the city limits. Reluctantly, they restrained their conversation to occasional whispers so they wouldn't distract Pete, who expertly pulled into the dentist's office ten minutes before Sarah's appointment.

"Do you care if we do a few errands while you have your appointment?" Pete turned to look at Sarah after parking.

"Sure. Do what you want to do. I'll call or text you when I'm finished. I don't think it will take long. Maybe about an hour, but don't hurry. I can wait for you in the waiting room."

Millie moved to the front seat while Sarah walked into the large waiting area and checked in. There were so many dentists in this practice, and she couldn't remember who she usually saw for her yearly appointment. Since this was an emergency appointment, she doubted it would be a dentist she'd seen before.

Sarah sat in the fashionable but slightly uncomfortable chair and twisted her face trying to make the pain materialize but worried at the same time it would prevent her from talking to the dentist if it emerged. The perky dental assistant called her name and led her into a cubicle, where she noted the information Sarah told her in response to her questions.

A young man breezed in and introduced himself as her dentist for the day. Sarah wondered if she was old enough to be his grandmother, but she liked his friendly manner and told him about her jaw pain. With his mask covering part of his face, he leaned in close and listened to her. She imagined she was looking at Sam when they were newlyweds because he had the same empathetic, friendly demeanor and sparkling, sky-blue eyes, and she felt safe and relaxed with him.

He looked at her teeth and ran his fingers along her jaw stopping at the joint and asked her to open and close her mouth and then bite her teeth together. Finally, he asked her to bite what looked like a roll of firmly wrapped cotton pads. As often as she tried, Sarah could not induce any pain, and she began to worry that he would think she was inventing her pain.

"I'm sorry. I don't know why it doesn't hurt now." Sarah

looked apologetically once more into the dentist's blue eyes, but she saw only compassion.

"Don't worry about it. I don't think there is anything wrong with your teeth, but if you have any other questions, give us a call. We'll help you figure it out." The young man smiled kindly at her as he helped her out of the chair and guided her toward the waiting room.

Sarah didn't see Pete's vehicle in the parking lot, so she called Millie to let her know she was finished and would wait for them on the bench inside the door. While she waited, she read a brochure about TMD which seemed to describe symptoms similar to hers. She was so engrossed in the information that she didn't notice Pete's SUV until Millie approached the doors. Sarah stuffed the pamphlet into her purse and opened the door before her friend reached it.

TANNA HEARD Jaz and Tucker racing down the hall before the high school students had finished pulling on their coats and retrieving their backpacks from their lockers after school. She heard a few good-natured greetings from some of her students who knew Jaz and Tucker, but they were not distracted. It was obvious they were determined to accomplish something.

Tucker burst into the room first and looked around the room. "Mommy, where's Vonnie?" Jaz followed on his heels and looked at Tanna for an explanation.

"Vonnie wasn't in school today, so you'll have to wait until tomorrow." Tanna was as disappointed as her children, but she did what she could to encourage them. "Maybe, Jesus wants you to wait for some reason."

Tanna hoped her children, especially Tucker, wouldn't detect her doubts about the situation. *What will Vonnie do with the little New Testament? She might just leave it behind like the class notes I tried to give her.*

"Who wants to play a computer game while I finish my work?" Tanna hoped she could distract her children while she gained control of her own doubts and misgivings, but Tucker and Jaz couldn't agree on a game to play, so she decided to break her own rules and let them watch a video on her phone.

Feeling frazzled, Tanna wanted nothing more than to lock herself in a room by herself and have a long heart to heart with God. Instead, she completed her tasks and gained control of her emotions before walking her children to her mom's house.

CHAPTER TWELVE

Tanna's cell phone rang after supper as she was transferring the casserole leftovers to a resealable container. Expecting it to be Sarah, she asked Jaz to answer it. "Tell Grammy there's plenty of casserole left if they're hungry."

Jaz looked puzzled after she answered the phone. "Somebody wants to talk to you, Mommy. It's not Grammy."

"Hello?" Tanna pressed the phone to her ear and drew her eyebrows together.

"Um… This is Vonnie. Can I ask you a question about the writing assignment you gave me?"

"Sure. Just hold on for a minute." Tanna muted her phone and motioned for Jaz to stand by her. "Will you read a story to Tucker in my bedroom?"

"Do I have to? He always talks when I read to him."

"Jaz, I'm helping a student with an assignment, and I have to concentrate. You can lie on my bed while you read, and I'll give each of you a cookie when I'm finished. Will you do that please?"

Jaz didn't answer Tanna. She just grabbed Tucker's arm and told him she would read him a story, and then they could have a cookie. Tucker's eyes widened, and he looked at

Tanna for confirmation. She nodded her head, and both of her children ran to her bedroom.

"Close the door, please," Tanna called to them and returned to her call. "Is everything all right, Vonnie? I missed you in school today." Tanna held her breath, hoping she wasn't asking Vonnie for too much information.

"I'm okay. It was kinda crazy around here today. My cousin came home, so lots of relatives were here, but what I wondered is how long that composition paper has to be. You know, the one you gave me when I was in your room with Tucker after school. I asked for the notes for *Romeo and Juliet*. You said I was missing a writing assignment... The one about games."

"Oh, yes. It should be at least one page long, but the most important thing is to cover the subject. You know, for example, if you are going to explain what you learned from a game like tic-tac-toe or most computer games, then you would explain that planning ahead is important. Also, describe what happens when you don't plan ahead in both the game and in life. Remember to relate it to life." Tanna paused, expecting Vonnie to either ask another question or tell her that she understood. When Vonnie didn't say anything, Tanna asked if she was still there.

"Yeah, I just don't think I can get this done by Friday."

The laughing and talking in the background of Vonnie's call made it difficult for Tanna to understand her. "I'm not sure what you said, but if you need more time, I'll let you wait until Monday. Will that help?"

"Yeah. I'm not even sure I'll be in school the rest of the week, but I can probably be done Monday. We can write about any game? Like a computer game or monopoly and stuff like that?"

"Yes, any game. It could be Sudoku, a crossword puzzle, a board game, or something similar. Okay?"

"Yeah, I think I got it. Bye."

"Vonnie… Vonnie?" As soon as Vonnie hung up, Tanna wished she had told her to stop in her room after school tomorrow, but then she remembered that Vonnie might not be there until Monday.

With a sigh, Tanna leaned back in her chair and absentmindedly picked up the newspaper lying on the end table. It was folded to the puzzle page. "What can I learn about life from a crossword puzzle? If I make one mistake, it messes up the whole thing? That sounds kind of cynical. But, if I write the answers with a pencil, I can learn from my mistakes and correct them. That's better. What else? Figuring out one part helps me find other answers." Tanna smiled. "I think I'm on a roll here. Let's see… Insisting an answer is right, when it isn't, leads to failure. Boy, do I know that from experience."

The phone rang, startling Tanna. "Hello."

"Tanna, I forgot to call before we left Bismarck, and the cell service is kind of spotty on that lonesome country road, so I couldn't get a signal until now. We should be there in about half an hour."

Tanna could hear Pete's voice in the background. "Tell her we want some coffee when we get there."

"Did you hear that, Tanna?"

"Tell Pete it'll be ready. Does he want decaf?"

"Pete, do you want decaf?"

"Tell Tanna I don't drink fake coffee." Tanna could hear Pete's hearty laughter.

"Okay. I'll make it strong enough to keep him up all night."

Tanna could hear muffled conversation before Sarah told

her Millie would have tea. "It's in that blue jar on the counter. Do you know where I mean?"

"I'll heat some water after I make the coffee, and you can find the tea for Millie when you get here. See ya soon."

"Thanks. And, Tanna, take some cookies out of the freezer, too."

JAZ WAS FINISHING a book when Tanna walked into her bedroom. "Millie and Pete are coming home with Grammy for coffee and cookies. You can have your cookies then, too, but you'll have to brush your teeth and go to bed after you finish. Do you want to put on your pajamas before they come?"

"No!"

"Yes!"

"Who said yes?"

"I did." Jaz raised her hand.

"And Tucker, why don't you want to put on your pajamas?"

"Well, Pete might think I look like a little kid."

Jaz put her hand on her forehead and rolled her eyes. "You *are* a little kid, Tucker."

"It sounds like they're already here, so you can have your cookies and then put on your pajamas."

"Do we have to come out of the bedroom in our pajamas?"

"No, Tucker, you can just go to bed. No one will see your pajamas unless you show them."

Tucker ran out with a big grin to open the door and held

it for the three smiling adults who entered and hung up their coats.

"Thank you, young fella." Pete held out his hand to shake Tucker's hand and then wouldn't let go of it.

"Pete! We gotta go have some cookies." Tucker giggled while he pulled Pete into the kitchen.

JAZ AND TUCKER reluctantly went to bed after listening to Pete tell them stories about his days as a cowboy on the range.

"Your grandpa and I spent a lot of nights under the stars when we were your age." Pete winked at Tucker, and Millie patted his arm while she shook her head.

"Every time you tell that story, you take a few years off your age. Pretty soon you'll be a baby strapped to the saddle. I think we better go home and let these folks go to bed."

Sarah walked with Pete and Millie to the door. "Thank you so much for driving to my appointment today, Pete. I don't know if I'll ever feel safe driving to Bismarck on my own. Sam always drove whenever we went there. It's a long way to drive with spotty cell phone service and no towns for miles."

"We were happy to do it, Sarah. Let's do it again, soon. At our age, we have appointments at least once a month!" Millie and Sarah hugged while Pete pulled on his coat.

Pete went out to start the SUV so it could warm up while Millie said her goodbyes to Sarah and Tanna. "We'll see you and the little ones on Saturday, Sarah. Why don't you plan to come for lunch before Pete takes the kids snowmobiling."

"That sounds like a good idea. I'll call Saturday morning

before we leave here. Thanks again for taking me to Bismarck." Sarah walked with her to the door and leaned out to wave at Pete.

Tanna was finishing the kitchen clean up when Sarah returned. "It looks like you had a good day with Millie and Pete, Mom."

Sarah nodded and avoided looking directly at Tanna while she began to meticulously wipe the kitchen counters that Tanna had just wiped. When she finished, she looked up and saw Tanna waiting with her arms crossed. "When are you going to tell me what's really going on?"

Sarah pursed her lips before she sat down at the table and began with tears in her voice. "There's not much to tell. I've had a sharp pain along my jaw. The physician's assistant at the clinic thought it might be a dental problem, but the dentist couldn't find anything wrong."

Tanna caressed Sarah's arm. "Mom, I had no idea you were having a problem. Maybe you need to go to a medical doctor in Bismarck. I could take time off to take you, and I'm sure Josh would come into town and stay with the kids after school. Are you in pain right now?"

Sarah shook her head. "The pain just randomly happens. Maybe I should check at the clinic in the morning. They could probably suggest a doctor in Bismarck. It's just so frustrating because I feel like the doctor or dentist thinks it's all in my head when I go to them, and the pain has just disappeared."

Tanna grasped her mom's folded hands. "We'll figure this out. Do you want me to stay home from school tomorrow?"

Sarah's eyes glistened when she looked up at her daughter. "Sam would know what to do. He always knew what was best for me, but I'm glad you're here. There's nothing we can

My Portion Forever

do about it tonight, so you better go to bed, and I'll go back to the clinic in the morning. Oh, and you heard Millie say that Pete will take the kids snowmobiling on Saturday so you and Josh can have some time together. That's important, too. Now, go to bed. I'll be fine."

After Tanna reluctantly went to bed, Sarah sat at her computer for an hour, researching the information from the pamphlet she had found at the dentist's office.

She read to herself: "Problems with your jaw and the muscles in your face that control it are known as temporomandibular disorders or TMD. This joint (TMJ) is the hinge that connects the jaw to the temporal bones of the skull which are in front of each ear. It enables the up-and-down and side-to-side movement needed for talking, chewing, and yawning. Dentists believe symptoms arise from problems with the muscles of your jaw or with the parts of the joint itself. The cause of TMD is unknown, but injury to the jaw, the joint, or the muscles of your head and neck can lead to TMD."

Sarah stopped reading to reflect on any accident she may have had that injured her jaw. There was the time she had attempted to help Sam with one of the horses that had an injured leg. Sam had just cautioned her to be careful because the flies were bothering the mare. As soon as he cautioned her, the horse violently threw her head to the side in an attempt to shake off the biting flies and smacked into the side of Sarah's face leaving her with a bruised cheek. Sarah chuckled to herself when she recalled how worried Sam had been that Sarah's dad would hold him responsible.

"Sam, you did it again. You found the answer for me!"

Convinced that she had found the answer, Sarah started

to shut down her computer but stopped to look for possible remedies for TMJ.

Sarah scanned the symptoms again looking for treatments. An overbite was mentioned which applied to her, and her jaw joint sometimes clicked when she chewed or opened and closed her mouth. Grinding or clenching her teeth was also something she periodically caught herself doing. The treatment list was long and involved various procedures to relieve individual symptoms. Some required dental procedures and others involved medication and exercises.

Frustration made her close her computer. "I can talk myself into all these symptoms if I try. I just want to know how to fix it. Sam, I need you!" Sudden tears trickled down Sarah's cheeks as she let despair and fear overwhelm her.

I'm here.

I know. Tell me what to do.

Trust Me.

How will that help me?

Trust Me.

I trust You to heal me. Is that what You want?

Sarah sat in silence, waiting for an answer, but she gave up and went to bed wondering if she had heard God or just imagined it. She fell asleep, planning to talk to the Physician's Assistant at the clinic about TMD.

CHAPTER THIRTEEN

Tanna found a message to call the high school office when she turned on her classroom computer on Thursday morning. When she returned the call, the principal made an appointment to discuss a parent complaint.

"Now what?" Tanna thought of any students she had disciplined this week and couldn't come up with anything that wasn't justified—at least to her. Students often thought she was too exacting with her assignments and rules, but overall, she thought everything had been going well. It wouldn't surprise her if a student had reported a problem to his or her parents that was a diversion for a missed or incomplete assignment.

As her first period students began to filter into the room, she reminded herself to put her problem aside. This was a happy day because tomorrow night she would go home and spend time with her husband. That reminded her that she'd have to explain to Tucker and Jaz tonight that they couldn't go home with her until Saturday.

Her first period class went smoothly, and she checked those students off the list of possible sources of the complaint. After she reminded them their writing assignment was due the next day, they groaned and asked for more time. Remembering the extension she had given Vonnie, she agreed to postpone the due date until Monday.

All three morning classes passed quickly. She looked at each of the students while they worked on their assignments, wondering who had a grievance against her. Finally, she made her way to the principal's office, feeling an uneasy sense of foreboding.

"Hello, Tanna. Thanks for coming in." The principal smiled as he closed the door to his office.

Tanna anxiously watched the principal open a folder which she assumed held the complaint. He handed her a sheet of notebook paper covered with writing and waited for her to read it. The mother of one of her students basically said her daughter was failing because Tanna was unwilling to help her.

```
When my daughter asks you for help you
make fun of her and tell her she's
lazy. Cindy is not lazy she just has
learning problems but you don't care
about that. You spend all your time
helping students who don't need it. If
Cindy wants to get help after school
you are always too busy. Thats your
job that you get payed for so why
don't you do it?
```

Tanna looked incredulously at the principal. "Did Cindy's mother talk to you about this? Because, I just saw her at the post office yesterday, and she was as friendly as always."

"Actually, it came in the mail yesterday. I wanted to talk

My Portion Forever

to you about it before I called her. Do you want me to set up a meeting?"

"Yes! Absolutely. And invite Cindy, too. I want to know why she thinks I won't help her and why she thinks I called her lazy. I would never intentionally call one of my students a disparaging name." Tanna paused to reflect for a moment. "I have warned the class as a whole that they won't earn good grades by being lazy. Maybe that was a mistake. I didn't mean to insult anyone."

"I'm sure you know as well as I do that students often misinterpret our words. I'll call and schedule a meeting to see if we can resolve this. Don't worry about it." The principal closed the folder, and Tanna felt like she was being dismissed.

Tanna stopped before she opened the office door. "I have Cindy in class after lunch, and I'll ask her if she needs help with anything. But I ask that at the end of most classes with little response." Tanna raised her shoulders and smiled quickly before leaving.

The first thing Tanna did when she returned to her classroom was look at Cindy's grades. They were not outstanding. There were several empty spaces for missing assignments, but her current average was passing. If the missing assignments turned into zeroes, she would fail, but Tanna usually let students hand in late work with the understanding that points would be deducted.

The bell rang, and Tanna quickly ate the protein bar she had brought for lunch. She was on the schedule for noon duty, so there wasn't much time to spare.

A few students had already gathered in the commons area when Tanna arrived. They chose to eat their sack lunches there after picking up a carton of chocolate milk in the cafeteria. Other students had finished the hot lunch served that day and were trickling out of the lunch room. Some sat on the few benches provided, while others stood or sprawled out on the floor.

Tanna's job was to maintain order and prevent students from leaving the building or going to the classrooms. Occasionally, she had to remind a couple to tone down their displays of affection. It usually wasn't a difficult job unless a fight broke out between two or more students. If that happened, Tanna sent a student for the principal or dean of students. Often, some of the male teachers were nearby and helped by separating the combative students. If she thought she could handle the situation, Tanna tried to stop the hostility, but she knew her limits.

Today was a quiet lunch period because everyone's favorite menu item, pizza, was being served, and many were enjoying seconds in the cafeteria. Before the bell rang, a group of boisterous boys approached the doors where Tanna stood. "Relax! You still have five more minutes. Why are you guys so anxious to go to class?"

When the boys laughed and walked away, Billy, who had been leaning against the wall close to Tanna, smiled. "Don't worry, Mrs. S! I got your back."

"Thanks, Billy. That's what I needed to hear today." Tanna exhaled when the bell rang, and she stepped aside as students crowded through the doorway to return to class.

SARAH WOKE with a start and looked around the room. *What day is it, and where am I?* It only took a moment for her to realize it was Thursday afternoon, and she'd fallen asleep on the couch after returning from the clinic.

They had scheduled an MRI for her tomorrow in Riverside, and she was a little concerned about it. The PA had given her a mild sedative to take before the scan after she admitted that she was mildly fearful of tight spaces. Waiting wasn't an option because the MRIs were only available once a month at the small-town hospital. Now, she had to find someone who would drive for her, but she was hopeful that she would finally know what was wrong.

As she struggled to recall everything the PA had told her today, her mind roamed to a dream she had been having when she had struggled to wake from her nap. The memory of it came in bits and disjointed pieces. Sam was there, and Matt was a part of it, too. The pleasant memory brought a smile but turned to confusion when she recalled that Sam and Matt had been arguing. Why? It had seemed so clear when she opened her eyes, but now it seemed jumbled and sad. Sarah closed her eyes and prayed for a lucid recollection.

Nothing came to mind while she quietly looked around the room until her gaze landed on a vacation picture taken at Mount Rushmore more than twenty years ago. Matt and Tanna had jumped out of the car so Sarah could snap a picture with the monument in the distance. A passing car, overflowing with suitcases, could be seen in the distance. Sarah sat up straighter. There had been a large suitcase in her dream, and Sam had refused to let anyone carry it except Sarah.

Her brow furrowed as she closed her eyes, attempting to pry open that tightly closed section of her memory, but her dream hovered, just out of reach. Why would Sam refuse to let anyone carry the heavy suitcase for her? Sam had been the consummate gentleman. He had never gone through a door without holding it open for her and letting her exit first. He had always started their vehicle so it was warm before she entered it, and he had never allowed her to carry something heavy if he was with her.

Sarah smiled when she remembered the argument Sam and Pete had often had about which set of cowboy rules they followed: Roy Rogers or Gene Autry? Both of them advocated respect and courtesy. Then, why wouldn't he carry her suitcase?

What does it mean, Lord?

Sarah threw back her head and stared at the ceiling. What had she dreamed the other day? She was lost in thought when the phone rang. "Hello."

"Sarah, it's Josh."

"Josh, how are you?"

"Not the best today. I'm having trouble with the starter on my tractor, and I really hope it will last through the winter."

"Oh, I'm sorry to hear that. You're not thinking about cancelling your weekend plans, are you?"

"No. I hope not, but I called to talk to you. What are your plans tomorrow? I'd like to talk to you about something."

"I have an appointment in Riverside tomorrow morning. Maybe you could take me, and we could talk on the way if it isn't too much trouble. If you can't, I can find someone else."

"Um, that should work. What time is your appointment?"

"It's at eleven tomorrow morning, so we'll have to leave here around ten. Will that give you enough time to do your chores?"

"I'm feeding the cows in the evening now, so that's not a problem."

"Sam did that, too, because he wanted the cows to have their calves during the day. It's a lot easier to check on cows and help them in the daylight."

"I'll be there in the morning. And, uh, Sarah, don't tell Tanna I want to talk to you. I'll explain everything to her tomorrow night."

"I won't say a word about it, but is it all right to tell her you're taking me to my appointment?"

"Oh, sure. That's not a problem."

"I'll see you tomorrow. Take care of yourself, Josh."

"Don't worry. I am."

Sarah's eyes widened as she turned off the phone. *I am! The words the Lord used when He told her it was time to let Sam go.*

Opening her Bible to the book of Exodus, Sarah glanced through the first two chapters until she found what she was searching for in the third chapter. God told Moses in verse 14, "I AM WHO I AM. When you go to the people of Israel, tell them, 'I AM sent me to you.'"

Sarah sat quietly for a few moments with her head bowed and her hands clasped in her lap. "You are and always have been enough, Lord. I loved Sam with all my heart, but I let myself believe he could supply all my needs. I didn't need You, Lord, because I had Sam."

Sarah slipped to the floor on her knees and wept for everything she had given up for both of them when she put all her trust in Sam.

"Forgive me, Lord, for squandering Your gift of freewill by accepting whatever Sam decided because it was easier than bearing the consequences of my own choices. Why didn't I help Sam carry that burden? I saw the pain I inflicted by deferring to him even when I knew he wanted me to seek

Your will, Lord. He was never meant to fulfill the desires of my heart; only You can do that. Forgive me for putting that burden on Sam and not giving it to You. I didn't allow him to be the gift You created for me. He was meant to be my beloved partner, not my god."

Sarah underlined the verses in her Bible, and holding a finger between the pages, she let her Bible fall open where there was a bookmark. She scanned the page, wondering why she had placed the marker there. The underlined verses were from Psalm 73. *(NRSV)*

> *[25] Whom have I in heaven but you?*
> *And there is nothing on earth that I desire other than you.*
> *[26] My flesh and my heart may fail,*
> *but God is the strength of my heart and my portion forever.*

As she often did, Sarah reached for another translation to be sure the words meant what she thought they did. *The Passion Translation* of Psalm 73:25 and 26 verified her thoughts.

> *[25]Whom have I in heaven but you? You're all I want!*
> *No one on earth means as much to me as you.*
> *[26]Lord, so many times I fail; I fall into disgrace.*
> *But when I trust in you, I have a strong and glorious presence protecting and*
> *anointing me. Forever you're all I need!*

Sarah smiled and held her Bible against her heart. "Thank You."

CHAPTER FOURTEEN

Tanna tried to call the high school principal after school, but his line was busy, so she walked to his office. Anxious to hear if he had connected with Cindy's mom, she stepped into his outer office and greeted the secretary.

"How's it going, Tanna?" The secretary was a hardworking woman who had been a few classes ahead of Tanna in school. "Are you still living in town with your mom?"

"Yes, there's still no electricity at the ranch, so Josh is roughing it without us."

"How's your mom? The secretary leaned forward and whispered, "Someone came in today and said they saw her at the clinic."

"Small towns! You gotta love 'em. Everybody knows everybody and everything." Tanna laughed, hoping the principal would come out of his office before the secretary could ask more questions, and on cue, he opened his office door.

"Tanna, come on in."

After hearing that the principal had not been able to contact Cindy's mother, Tanna left the office and walked by the secretary with a wave. "See you tomorrow."

The clock on Tanna's classroom wall told her she could pack up what she needed and go home, but something was lying on her desk. It was a piece of notebook paper with Vonnie's distinct handwriting on it. Tanna glanced out the door before she picked up the note.

```
I don't have a computer I can use at
my grandmas house because my cousin
and his friend are always on it so I
couldn't look up any computer games so
I wrote this poem about games people
play. I hope its ok.
```

Games People Play
By Vonnie Lynch

I'm new at this game called family
And no one here will teach me how to play.
Just give it time
They say.

Why don't they understand?
The wonder, the uncertainty, the fears
Are all new to me
And worst of all the tears.

Sometimes when I'm tired of trying to win
I send the game crashing to the floor
Only to pick up the shattered pieces
And want to try once more.

TEARS welled in Tanna's eyes as she reread the poem. *Lord, how can I help this troubled student? There's a hurting little girl inside of her.*

Footsteps approached her door, and she brushed the tears from her eyes as Monica hesitantly walked in the door. "Are you busy?"

"No, not really. I'm just reading a paper Vonnie dropped off here. Did you see her go by your room a little while ago?"

"Yes, she looked kind of different when I saw her walking down the hall. Her hair was really plain, you know, not fixed up like it usually is, and she didn't look like she had on any makeup. She still looked pretty, but young—a lot younger without her makeup and trendy hairdo. I wonder what's up?"

Tanna shrugged one shoulder. "I'm sorry I missed her. I'd like to know when she'll be back in school."

Before Monica could launch into her latest gossip monologue, Tanna asked her about her new boyfriend.

Monica waved her hand. "Oh, I don't think it's going to work out with him. We just don't want the same things. How did you ever catch someone as nice and good looking as that husband of yours?" Monica raised her eyebrows and laughed self-consciously. "I didn't mean that he's not a lucky man to have you, too. I just wanna know how you found the right one. You know what I mean?"

Tanna considered telling her about the other Josh in her past, but she didn't want to add anything to Monica's cache of gossip. Until recently, the "other Josh" hadn't even crossed Tanna's mind.

"I'm not sure I found the right one." Tanna waited for Monica's mouth to drop open. "I didn't find him, and he didn't find me. God brought us together."

"You mean, you didn't have a choice? You just had to do what God told you to do? And how did He tell you? Was it like God sent a message somehow that said, 'He's the one?'"

Monica's doubtful expression made Tanna wonder if she had time to adequately finish this conversation before Jaz and Tucker would give up waiting for her in the library and rush into her room ready to leave for the day.

"God speaks to me in lots of different ways. Sometimes, He whispers an idea or thought in my heart. Other times, I understand that He is speaking to me when I read the Bible or listen to our pastor in church. There are even times when God speaks to me through my children or friends. I think having a personal relationship with God is the best way to hear from Him on a regular basis, though. Would you be interested in going to church with us sometime?"

"I don't know. Maybe. Do you think God will show me who to marry if I go to church?"

An idea popped into Tanna's mind, but she had to act quickly. "Would you like a Bible, Monica? I have a small book here that has part of the Bible in it. Some passages are marked if you want to read them. It's the best way to know God and His son, Jesus." Tanna opened her desk drawer and took out the New Testament that was waiting for Tucker to give to Vonnie.

"I guess I could." Monica took the small Bible and awkwardly shifted her weight from one foot to the other. "I better go now. I have some papers to correct."

Tanna had never seen Monica so anxious to leave. Maybe she should have approached her differently. Did she expect Monica to accept too much too quickly? *Show me what to do, Lord, for both Monica and Vonnie.*

Tanna gathered her coat and purse. It was time to go home and make more definite plans for the weekend. Maybe her mom would have some ideas about what she should have said to Monica.

CHAPTER FIFTEEN

Friday morning, Tanna woke feeling happy and excited, but it was short-lived when she walked into her children's room and found Tucker coughing and crying. Sitting on the bed, she pulled him onto her lap. "What's wrong, buddy?"

Tucker turned his tear-filled eyes to her. "Mommy, I don't feel good." His statement was promptly followed by him losing everything in his tummy.

"Eww." Jaz climbed down from her top bunk and plugged her nose.

"Jaz, bring me a wet washcloth and towel, and tell Grammy Tucker is sick."

After changing Tucker into clean clothes, Tanna carried him to the living room and sat with him on the couch. Sarah brought in a small pail for him to use if he felt sick again and helped Jaz prepare for school.

While Jaz ate her breakfast, Tanna asked her mom to bring her the phone. "I better call before it's too late to find a substitute for me, and will you walk Jaz to school?"

After Sarah handed her the phone, Tanna spoke with the high school secretary and told her where to find her emergency lesson plans. She also asked her to call the preschool teacher and tell her Tucker wouldn't be there.

"I can stay home with Tucker if you want me to, Tanna. I know you don't like to miss school."

"Mom, your appointment is important. Tucker and I will have a good day together. Won't we?" Tucker snuggled into her arms and closed his eyes. "After Josh brings you home, we'll see if we have to change our plans for tomorrow."

"Nooo! I wanna go snowmobiling. Grammy and I can go without Tucker."

Tanna hadn't noticed Jaz waiting in the doorway, holding her coat and backpack. "Jaz, there will be other days for snowmobiling. Let's not worry about it for now."

Tanna looked at Jaz with pleading eyes, and Sarah touched Jaz's arm. "Are you ready? It'll just take me a minute to put on my coat."

TANNA WAS STILL HOLDING Tucker when Josh came to pick up Sarah. He still felt a little feverish, but there had been no more nausea.

"Hey there, little man. You're not feeling so good, huh?" Tucker's lower lip trembled as Josh lifted him from Tanna's arms. He buried his head between Josh's neck and shoulder, and Josh clutched him tightly. Tanna could hear the soft murmur of Josh's words as he rocked his son to sleep. She gestured for Josh to follow her to the kitchen after he gently lowered Tucker onto the couch.

"I could take Mom to Riverside if you want to stay here with Tucker."

"I would, but there are some things I need to do in Riverside. Maybe I could come back tonight after I feed the cattle. I won't be able to stay overnight because I have to keep a fire going in the woodstove, especially after the sun goes down. Do you think he'll feel good enough for you to go home with me?"

"I don't know. I might call the clinic and see what they say about him." Tanna stepped closer to Josh and wrapped her arms around his waist. His arms enfolded her, and she rested her head against his chest. "I've missed you."

Josh lifted her chin with his fingertips. "There'll be another time if it doesn't work out this weekend."

Reluctantly, Josh released Tanna and walked to the door to put his coat on before holding the door open for Sarah, who discreetly waited in the hallway.

SARAH HAD no idea the MRI would be so loud. In her research, she'd read that some people like to bring some soothing music to listen to during the procedure, so she brought some praise music with her, but she struggled to hear it above the din of the machine. She didn't realize she was dozing until the technician told her she was finished. As she took off her hospital gown, she prayed that this test would reveal the cause for the spasms of intense pain.

Josh was waiting for her after she changed into her own comfortable slacks and sweater. He asked if she was ready for lunch, and she was surprised that she was actually hungry. It was a feeling she seldom noticed lately.

Sarah ordered the special of the day at her favorite restaurant in Riverside. A large family ran it, and they specialized in homemade meals and soups. It had been Sam's favorite place to eat, and Sarah always took leftover food home from their abundant servings.

The special today was a Reuben sandwich with creamy knoephla soup. Everyone in the area made knoephla soup a little differently, but the soup at this restaurant tasted the most like the soup her mother had made, so Sarah was always happy to see it on the menu. Josh had never developed a taste for the rich German soup made with potatoes, dumplings, cream, onions, and chicken bouillon, so he ordered a hamburger and chili, the other soup of the day.

Before their food came, Josh asked Sarah about her MRI. She confessed that the only thing she remembered was the loud clanging of the machine. "It must have been the mild sedative I took before my appointment. I wasn't really aware that I was sleeping until they woke me."

The friendly and chatty waitress brought their soup and told them their meals would be ready shortly. They bowed their heads, and Josh uttered a quick but heartfelt prayer of thanks for Sarah's test and the food they were about to eat. Before he finished, he added a request for answers to her health challenges and healing for Tucker.

After they blew on their first spoonfuls of soup and carefully tasted them, Sarah cocked her head and looked directly at Josh. "What's on your mind?"

Josh dropped his gaze to his bowl of chili and placed the spoon on his napkin. "I don't know where to start." After an awkward moment, Sarah continued to eat her soup, and Josh rubbed his jaw. "You probably know that Tanna and I are having some problems."

Sarah pursed her lips, but she didn't say anything. Josh ate more of his chili, but he didn't make eye contact with Sarah. Finally, he looked at her with glistening eyes. "I know she's not happy. You must know, too. She always told me she can't hide anything from you, but this isn't about Tanna. Well… um…it is…but…uh…there's more to it."

The amiable waitress brought their food and asked if they needed anything else. After Sarah shook her head, Josh asked for more water.

"Let's just eat our food, and then we can finish our conversation." Josh waited for Sarah to agree and waited for the waitress to fill his glass.

They finished their meal in silence, interrupted only once by an acquaintance who stopped at their table as she was leaving the restaurant. The friend of Sarah's tried to prod her into saying why she was in Riverside with her son-in-law, but she simply answered that they both had errands there, so they came together.

Josh finished his burger, and Sarah asked for a to-go box for half of her sandwich after she insisted on paying the bill, including the tip.

"Do you want to finish our conversation here or in the pickup?"

After glancing around the crowded restaurant, Josh stood. "Let's finish in the pickup. Okay?"

Sarah stood and Josh helped with her coat. She continued to talk as they walked outside the restaurant. "I think tomorrow is going to be a nice day, so I hope the kids and I can go snowmobiling with Pete." Sarah paused as Josh opened the pickup door for her. After they were settled in their seats, she turned to face Josh. "Whatever you have to tell me won't change how I feel about you. Tanna is right. She usually can't hide things from me, so I know you are a good man. I'm ready to help however I can."

Josh grasped the steering wheel with both hands and

hung his head before raising it to face Sarah. "The last time we visited you and Sam that Christmas before..."

"Yes. I remember. And I'm thankful Sam and I could spend his last Christmas with all of you. Sam was happier than I think I've ever seen him. I wonder if he knew his time was short." Sarah gave Josh a half smile when he turned to face her.

"This is about Sam and something he told me that day when I went out to the barn with him. I have to tell Tanna, but I wanted to tell you first." Josh reached out to touch Sarah's arm when he noticed the alarm on her face. "It's not bad, but it may surprise you."

"Please just say it, Josh. You're making me think all kinds of crazy things." Sarah grasped his hand and squeezed it.

Letting out his breath, Josh told her Sam had warned him not to try to take the place of God in Tanna's life. Struggling to find the words to continue, he hesitantly faced Sarah.

"There's obviously more so just say it, Josh." Sarah softened her words with a knowing smile. "Did Sam tell you that he thought he took the place of God in my life?" When Josh hesitated, Sarah continued. "It's true. He did, but not intentionally. He was very good at supplying all my needs and wants. Sometimes, I felt like a spoiled child because all I had to do was mention something, and if Sam could take care of it, he would. He wasn't a tyrant. He let me make my own decisions, but he always fixed it if I made a bad choice."

Before Sarah continued, Josh interrupted her with an apology. "I'm sorry I had to tell you that. I really hope Sam wouldn't care that I did."

"Josh, the Lord has been telling me the same thing. I wasn't blameless. I never had to regret making a bad decision because I let Sam make them for both of us. Sam did so much for me that I didn't know he'd taken God's place in my life until he..." Sarah struggled to continue.

"He loved you so much Sarah. You know that." Josh waited for Sarah to nod her head. "And I love Tanna, but I've made a mess trying to figure out how to use the advice Sam gave me. I think Tanna is disappointed in me most of the time."

"Tell her what you told me."

"But how do I tell her without destroying her image of your marriage? It's what I thought I had to live up to before Sam talked to me."

"Josh, I'm so sorry. Talk to her. Work it out together. I wish Sam and I had done that. Each of you has to say what you want from the other and be willing to compromise. I know Tanna can be stubborn, but you have to be honest even if she doesn't want to believe you. Tell her what Sam told you, and read Psalm 73:25 and 26. It'll be fine." Sarah patted Josh's shoulder and smiled. "I'll pray that God gives you the right words and that he softens Tanna's heart enough to understand them."

"Thank you."

"We should probably go before Jaz decides to walk home from school without us."

CHAPTER SIXTEEN

After dropping Sarah off at her house, Josh drove to the school to meet Jaz. He watched as waves of very young children, followed by junior high and high school students, exited the building to either fill into the buses or walk away. Sarah had offered to go, but Josh wanted to spend a little time with Jaz before he had to go home.

Soon some of the teachers could also be seen leaving the building to either walk home or go to their cars. The number of departing students dwindled, and he began to worry that Jaz had walked by without him noticing. She was probably at Sarah's house by now, and they would all wonder what happened to him. As he moved his cell phone trying to locate a signal, Jaz came out of the school with a teacher. Relieved, he opened his window and waved.

Jaz began to run toward him, but the teacher called her back and handed her a folder. By the time she climbed into the pickup, she was breathless. "Daddy! Is the electricity back?"

"No, sweetheart. I just got back from taking Grammy to an appointment. I wanted to see you before I go home." Josh reached out to hug his daughter. "How was school?"

"Okay." Jaz lifted her shoulder and pouted in her seat as they drove to Sarah's house.

Josh parked the pickup in Sarah's driveway and followed Jaz to the house. She flung open the door and dropped her coat and boots in the entry before rushing into the kitchen. Tanna looked up from her cup of tea at the table, and Sarah turned her head away from something she stirred in a pot on the kitchen range.

"Mommy, where's Tucker?" Jaz looked around the room.

"He's sleeping in my room. How was school?"

"Is he still sick? Will we be able to go snowmobiling tomorrow?"

Jaz's rapid questions prompted Tanna to stand and hold up one finger in her daughter's direction. "Slow down. I don't know yet if we'll go snowmobiling. Now, let me talk to Daddy for a minute."

"I can't stay long. It'll be dark soon, but I wanted to know how Tucker is feeling."

"I think he's much better than he was this morning, but he had a temperature all day, so I called the clinic. I guess there's a 24-hour something going around, so he probably has that. We'll have to see how tonight goes. Our weekend plans will have to be postponed."

Josh rubbed his jaw. He was sure his expression mirrored the disappointment he saw in Tanna's and Jaz's faces.

"If we're not going snowmobiling tomorrow, can't I go home with you, Daddy?" Jaz fixed her eyes on Josh and gripped his arm.

Josh pushed his hat back on his head and knelt in front of Jaz. "You remember that the electricity is off, right?"

"That's okay. We could roast marshmallows in the wood

My Portion Forever

stove before we go to bed. It would be so much fun, Daddy. Please."

"But, Honey, listen. You'll have to stay in the dark house by yourself while I feed the cattle. That'll be for about two hours." Josh held his daughter's gaze while he waited for her to answer.

"Can't I ride in the tractor with you?"

Josh rubbed his neck and jaw as he looked at Tanna for help.

"Jaz, how does this sound? If Tucker feels better tomorrow, we'll all go to the ranch together."

"But, Mommy, I want to go with Daddy now." Jaz's eyes filled with tears, and Tanna looked helplessly at Josh.

"I can't leave Tucker here with Mom. He's been clinging to me all day. We'll just have to make plans some other time for, you know, what we had planned." Sadness clouded Tanna's features.

Releasing his breath, Josh looked from Tanna to Jaz. "If you can get ready in five minutes, you can go with me, but remember there is no television or running water."

Jaz grabbed her backpack and coat. "Most of my clothes are still at home so let's go, Daddy!"

Josh gave Tanna a quick hug and followed Jaz to the door. "Call me tonight before you go to sleep."

TANNA STOOD in the doorway and sadly watched her husband and daughter drive away. *Lord, I thought this was our chance.*

Trust Me.

Tanna shivered and closed the door when she heard Tucker calling her.

"I'll be right there, Sweetie." Tanna gathered the Children's Tylenol and a glass of water before going to her bedroom where Tucker was sitting up on the bed. "Are you feeling better?" Tanna touched his face and thought he felt a little cooler. After giving him his medicine and watching him drink some of the water, she sat beside him.

Tanna had finished reading one of Tucker's favorite books to him when Sarah stuck her head in the door and announced that the soup was ready. "Do you want me to bring some in for both of you?"

"I think Tucker can sit by the table. Right?" Tanna eyed her son.

He crawled off the bed and started for the kitchen, but stopped when Tanna didn't follow him. "Aren't you hungry, Mommy?"

"Go ahead. I'll be right there." Tanna was sliding off the bed when her cell phone rang. The caller ID said Josh was the caller. "Did you forget something, Josh?"

"Mommy, it's me. I forgot to tell you that I saw that pretty girl today before I left the school. I don't remember her name. She was in your room after school that day with Tucker."

"Jaz, do you mean Vonnie? That high school girl Tucker talked to?"

"Yeah. Well, she asked me if you were in your room today, so I told her you were at Grammy's house. Then she said she wanted to talk to you, so I told her I would tell you, but I forgot."

"Did she say why she wanted to talk to me?"

Jaz was quiet for a moment. "I don't think so. I have to go

now. Daddy says supper is ready. We're roasting hot dogs! Bye."

Frowning as she started to turn off her phone, Tanna scrolled through the list of callers. There was her outgoing call to the clinic, but the only incoming calls today were from an unknown caller, so she deleted it. Scrolling back further, she searched for the call from Vonnie.

Was that Wednesday night? There were three calls on Wednesday from unknown callers, but only one matched the approximate time Vonnie had called. *Why didn't I save her number to my phone?* Tanna chided herself, but a disturbing thought made her mouth twist. *I probably deleted her call today without even thinking. Wait... I would have heard my phone ring... unless it was while I was in the bathroom with Tucker.*

"Argh!" Tanna shook her head. She slammed her fist on her thigh. "Why did I delete those calls without listening to them?"

"Tanna, what's wrong?" Sarah stood in the doorway with a concerned look on her face.

"Nothing. I just forgot to do something. Is Tucker eating?" Tanna put her phone down and walked toward her mom but stopped before leaving the room to go back and retrieve her phone.

Sarah waited for Tanna but watched her as she approached. Something was wrong, and Sarah hoped it didn't have anything to do with Josh.

Tucker was happily slurping the homemade noodles from Sarah's chicken noodle soup as they walked in the kitchen. "This is 'crumptious, Grammy!"

Leveling her gaze at Tucker, Tanna lifted his chin. "Use your 's' sounds, Tucker."

"*Scrumptious*, I mean." Tucker sheepishly turned to Sarah.

"Well, thank you. I'm glad you like it, but how did you learn a big word like 'scrumptious?'" Sarah's mouth curved into a smile.

Tucker shrugged his shoulders and hid a grin as he continued to devour his soup.

"Slow down, Kiddo. We don't want to upset your tummy again."

"I think these noodles like sliding into my tummy." Tucker swallowed another mouthful and suddenly looked agitatedly from Sarah to Tanna. "Where is Jaz?"

Scratching her head, Tanna dodged the question. "I think she's at home."

"Is she hiding?" Tucker glanced under the table and suspiciously eyed Tanna when she laughed.

"She went home with Daddy after school." Tanna waited for Tucker's reaction.

Tucker frowned. "Are they coming back?"

Looking desperately at her mom, Tanna searched for an explanation that wouldn't set off an outburst from her son. "They won't be back tonight, but we'll call Daddy as soon as you finish your soup. Would you like that?"

Tucker vigorously nodded his head, and Tanna hoped there wouldn't be a problem when they talked to Josh.

CHAPTER SEVENTEEN

Josh had to admit that having Jaz with him was a welcome distraction that stopped him from thinking about Tanna and the evening he had planned for them. After he and Jaz roasted their hot dogs and marshmallows on the fire in the wood stove, Tanna called so he could talk to Tucker, who was disappointed that he was in town instead of at the ranch. His son tried to talk him into coming to town so he could go back with him, but Josh told him he had to get completely well. Tucker had reluctantly agreed, but he thought Jaz was a "lucky duck."

"Where did you learn that expression, Tucker?"

Josh could hear Tanna telling their son, "Daddy can't hear you when you shrug your shoulders."

That started a game that Tucker and Josh played for five minutes.

"Guess what I'm doing now, Daddy?"

"Scratching your nose? No, wait, make that *picking* your nose."

"No, Mommy won't let me do that. Guess again, Daddy."

"Eating a carrot?"

"Daddy!"

"What?"

Tucker giggled. "You could hear me if I was eating a carrot."

"Okay. Rubbing your chin?"

"No. Do you give up?"

"That depends on what I win if I guess what you're doing? Will I win a new saddle?"

"I don't have enough money for a saddle, Daddy."

"What have you been spending all your money on—coffee at the gas station?"

"No." Tucker giggled.

"You better tell me what you're doing so I can talk to Mommy for a little while." Josh waited for an answer but heard only silence.

"Tucker? Are you still there?"

"I forgot what I was doing? It took you too long to guess, and I forgot."

"We both win then, and the prize I want is you! Is that a deal?

"Daddy! What do you want to do with me?"

"How about wrestle with you? That's what I want to do."

"Hmm… I think we could work that out, but don't forget."

"I won't, Tucker. I'm looking forward to it. Love you."

"Love you more."

After a short silence, Josh could hear Tanna telling Tucker to pick out some books. "I'll have to call you back later, Josh. It'll take me a while to get Tucker settled into bed because he slept a lot today. I think Mom will read to him while we talk, but first I want to make a quick call to one of my students who was looking for me today."

"That will give me time to get Jaz ready for bed and into

her pajamas. It looks like she zonked out on the couch while Tucker and I were talking."

"Why don't you just leave her on the couch? You know how hard it is to get her back to sleep if she wakes up. Just make sure there's some kind of light for her if she wakes in the night."

"Okay, where's a nightlight?"

Tanna laughed. "There are some battery-powered, fake candles on the sideboard. Just put fresh batteries in so they'll stay on all night. Where are you sleeping?"

"I think I'll sleep in our bedroom. If Jaz wakes, that's where she'll look for me. If I sleep somewhere else, she might freak out if she doesn't know where I am. I wish you were here."

"Me, too."

After a couple moments of silence, Josh told Tanna he'd talk to her later.

Tanna fingered her phone, trying to decide if she should call Vonnie.

"Mommy, we read all the books today. Now what are we gonna do?" Tucker tilted his head and smiled the half smile that told Tanna he had something in mind.

"What do you want to do, Tucker?"

Tucker flung out his hand with his fingers splayed and twisted his mouth. "Well, we could see if there's a kid show on TV..."

Tanna smiled and thought for a minute. "Put on your pajamas, and I'll see what Grammy has for kid shows."

Tanna was scrolling through the channels when Tucker, dressed in his cowboy pajamas, plopped on the couch. An old Tom and Jerry cartoon immediately captivated him so Tanna went to find Sarah.

"Mom, are you making cookies?"

"Just a few to take with us tomorrow if we go to Pete and Millie's. Tucker seems to feel well again, so I thought you might want to go to the ranch while the children and I go snowmobiling."

"I'm not so sure Tucker is over whatever he has, but we'll see how the night goes. He's busy watching cartoons now. Do you mind looking in on him occasionally while I make a phone call?"

"Sure. I just have one batch left to bake, and then I'll join him."

"Mom, thank you so much for all you've done for us. We really appreciate it." Tanna turned to leave the kitchen but stopped herself. "I know you told me that your MRI went well, but I didn't even ask you if they gave you any indication what is causing your pain." Tanna watched Sarah slide the sheet of freshly baked cookies out of the oven.

"They didn't tell me anything. The results will be in a report sent to the clinic, so I'll have to wait for them to get back to me." Sarah raised her eyebrows and smiled.

Tanna and Sarah walked out of the warm fragrant kitchen together, but Tanna left her mom with Tucker after retrieving her phone.

Closing the door behind her, Tanna sat on the bed and opened her cell phone. *I hope this isn't a mistake. Vonnie might not want to hear from me.* She found the old call from Vonnie and touched the number.

"Hello?"

"Vonnie, Jaz told me you were looking for me today. I'm sorry if I missed a call from you."

"Just a minute." Loud music played in the background,

and Tanna heard Vonnie yelling for someone to turn the music down.

A male voice bellowed back. "Who are you talking to?"

"Stay out of my business."

The phone sounded like it fell, but Tanna could still hear shouting until it faded into the background. After a few minutes, the phone went silent.

"Vonnie, are you still there? Vonnie?" Tanna waited before touching the off button and immediately hit recall, but the phone went to Vonnie's voice mail inbox.

"I don't know what happened, but call me if you need anything." Tanna said after the beep.

Tanna had an uneasy feeling, but she didn't know what to do about it except call her husband and ask him.

The phone rang five times before Josh answered.

"Hi! Sorry. I fell asleep waiting for you to call."

"I'm sorry it took so long, but I had a strange situation. Remember how I said I was going to call a student who was looking for me today?"

"Yup. Did you talk to her—or him?"

Tanna explained what happened and added that she was worried about Vonnie. "I left a message for her to call. Do you think I should try to find out what's going on?"

"Tanna, I think you've done what you can. For all you know, she dropped her phone in a sink full of water or her battery needs charging."

"You're probably right, but I can't get over this feeling that something is wrong."

"You aren't responsible for everyone. She has parents."

"No. Actually she doesn't. Well, she does, but she doesn't live with them. I'll just try and call her again later. There isn't much else I can do. Sometimes, I just wish I could bring these kids home with me."

"You'll let me know before you do that, won't you?"

"Don't worry. I don't think the school would approve. How are you and Jaz doing?"

"She's still sound asleep on the couch. She'll probably wake me up in the morning. How about Tucker?"

"He seems to feel fine, and I hope that continues through the night because Mom is still making plans to go to Pete and Millie's. If that works out, I could spend the afternoon at the ranch with you."

"Not exactly the weekend I had planned, but I'll take it. Would you all stay overnight?"

"I don't think so. I just don't know. We'll see how tomorrow goes. Okay?"

CHAPTER EIGHTEEN

After saying "good night" to Josh, Tanna walked into the living room where she found Sarah and Tucker both sleeping. She turned off the television and carried Tucker into his bed. She covered him and partially closed the door, mentally noting that she should leave her door ajar tonight, as well.

"Watch over him, Lord, and please heal his little body," Tanna whispered before returning to the living room.

Sarah passed Tanna in the hallway on the way to her bedroom. "I didn't know I was so tired. It's been a long day, so I'm going to shower and go to bed. Is there anything you need, Honey?"

"Thanks, Mom. I think I'll go to bed, too. We might have a busy day tomorrow. Do you want me to turn off the lights and lock the doors?"

"I think the doors are already locked, but you can turn off the lights. Oh, and the cookies are on the counter if you want one. I got a little carried away, so there are more than we need. Guess I forgot Tucker wouldn't be sampling them."

Tanna patted her mom's arm. "I could probably force myself to take over Tucker's job this one time. I feel like snacking on something, but I'm not sure what."

After drinking a cup of tea and eating two cookies, Tanna didn't feel satisfied, but she knew food wasn't the answer. Something pestered her, but she didn't know what to do about it. A quick check of her phone revealed no new messages or calls. She walked through the dining room to check on Tucker and noticed that her mom's light was off. Tucker was sleeping soundly, and his forehead felt cool as she brushed his hair to the side. *At least they're both getting some rest. What am I going to do?*

Suddenly, a long, hot bath sounded irresistible. She had just lowered herself into the bubbly, fragrant tub when the ring tone on her phone began to play. Groaning, she stretched out her wet arm, but the phone was just beyond her reach. It lay there on the bathroom rug, flashing and playing a lively Mozart sonata.

Grabbing her towel, Tanna stepped out of the tub and dried her hands. The words *Unknown Caller* flashed off the screen just as she lifted the phone from the floor.

"OH!" Covering her mouth, Tanna silenced her outburst. Waking her mom was the last thing she wanted.

Tanna quickly tapped the voicemail icon and listened to Vonnie's message. It was difficult to hear her whispers above the loud music playing, but the muffled words, "I can't do this," were clear. Tanna listened again with the same results.

What does Vonnie need help with? Why would she be working on an assignment now, and why would she be calling me this late? Tanna was certain Vonnie needed help, but with what? The knot in her stomach tightened as she pushed the recall button and waited. The call went straight to voicemail, and Tanna ended the call.

Help me, Lord. I don't know what to do. Is Vonnie just playing me for a fool? It wouldn't be the first time a student had prank-called her. That's why she usually turned her phone off after 11 p.m., but this felt different somehow.

Finally, she decided to access Vonnie's contact information through her teacher's school web account. The only contact listed for Vonnie was her aunt. Tanna copied the number but then realized it was the same number Vonnie had been using. They must share a phone, and Vonnie had it. *Now what? Who would know Vonnie's grandparents' names? Monica! She knows everybody and everything...but is it too late to call her?*

Tanna was tempted to forget the whole situation. Tomorrow, Vonnie would call with a simple question about *Romeo and Juliet,* and Tanna would wonder why she had overreacted. Everything would seem different in the light of day and after a good night's sleep, but she hesitated to turn her cell phone off. *What if something is wrong?*

Almost afraid that someone would answer, Tanna tried to call Vonnie again. This time she decided to leave a message, but the voicemail box was full. Tanna told herself it was time to give up and go to bed, but she couldn't do that. What could she do?

Leave a text.

Thank you, Lord.

Tanna closed her eyes and smiled before she started the text.

> What's going on? Are you all right? I'm sorry I missed your calls. Please, let me know if you need anything. I'm still awake, so I'm here if you need me.

Tanna read and reread the text message several times before deleting it and trying again with a simple message: *I'm here if you need me.* She still had the nagging feeling that she was being duped, but she couldn't stop herself from touching the send button.

As soon as she heard the woosh of the message sending, she wanted to stop it, but it was too late. When her phone rang, she fumbled to answer it.

"Hello."

"Tanna, it's me, Monica. I hope I'm not calling too late."

"No. I'm still awake, and I was just thinking about you."

"I've been thinking about you, too, ever since we talked the other day, and you gave me this Bible. I wanted to ask you about something I read, but you weren't in school today. That can wait, though, tell me why you were thinking about me."

"Well, I was just wondering if you have any idea how I could contact Vonnie's grandparents. They don't have a phone listing."

"I don't know, but can't you find contact information through your teacher login on the school web page?"

"That didn't help. Do you know where Vonnie's grandparents live?"

"Ah, yeah. They live in that big house across from the city park. The gray one. But I don't think they're home. I heard Vonnie talking to her cousin at the gas station after school—you know, her auntie's son, the one who just came home from rehab. He told her their grandparents had to go to Fargo to get his mom because her car broke down."

Tanna frowned. "So Vonnie's aunt and grandparents are gone?"

"That's what it sounded like unless they're back from Fargo. Why?"

"It just doesn't seem like a good idea to leave Vonnie

home alone." Tanna realized she was thinking out loud, and she really didn't want Monica to know she was concerned. "Oh, never mind, Vonnie's grandparents must have thought she'd be safe until they came home."

"Well, her cousin is there. He's nineteen and really a pretty decent kid—at least he was in high school. He just got mixed up with the wrong group after he graduated."

Tanna laughed. "Monica, I grew up in this community, but you know more about the people here than I do. Now, tell me what question you had for me. Was it something you read in the New Testament?"

"The New Testament?"

"You know that little Bible book I gave you. It's just the New Testament part of the Bible."

"There's another part?"

"Yes, there's a whole other part that starts with God creating the world. You've heard of Adam and Eve, haven't you?"

"Of course. Everybody knows that story, but I've never read it in a Bible, although it seems like my mom used to read stories to me from the Bible when I was little."

"Your mom could probably answer your questions, too. What did you read that you wanted to ask me about?"

Tanna could hear Monica yawn. "That's a good idea to ask my mom. She'd like that, and I haven't called her for a while."

Tanna's phone beeped that she had an incoming call. "Good night, Monica. I'll see you on Monday." Tanna's hand trembled as she tapped the accept call button. "Hello?" All Tanna heard was a faint but steady creaking sound. "Vonnie?"

"Will you tell Tucker I'm sorry?" Vonnie sniffed.

"Sorry for what? Vonnie, what's wrong? Where are you?"

"I tried… It's just too late for me."

"Vonnie? Where are you? Are your grandparents home?" Tanna walked to the window and looked out at the deserted street shrouded in the misty glow of the corner street lamp. "Where are you? Vonnie, talk to me."

"I bet you're a good mom. You'd never leave your kids to…" Vonnie's voice faded to a whisper.

"I can't hear you, Vonnie. Please, tell me where you are." Tanna tried to relax her grip on the phone and gasped when Sarah walked in the room. Shaking her head in response to her mom's questioning look, she tried again. "Vonnie, where are you?" Tanna looked helplessly at Sarah as the repetitive creak on the other end of the phone abruptly stopped and the line went dead.

"Mom, I have to find her." Tanna went to the coat rack and pushed her arms in the sleeves. "Do you care if I use your…"

Sarah wordlessly handed her the keys to her car. "Are you sure?"

Tanna nodded.

"Then be careful. I'll be praying."

CHAPTER NINETEEN

Lord, will you show me where to find her? Tanna pleaded while driving to Vonnie's grandparents' home. The house was dark, and Tanna sat in her car, struggling to decide if she should go to the door. She had never met anyone from Vonnie's family. How would she explain banging on their door in the middle of the night, demanding to know Vonnie's location?

Lord, I need some help here. I'm afraid for me and for Vonnie.
Listen.

Tanna held her phone to her ear. "Vonnie, I'm at your grandparents' house. Are you here? Do you need help?" All Tanna heard was the same repetitive creaking followed by a muffled sob. "Vonnie, I'm coming. I'll be at your door in a minute."

"No! Don't go there." Vonnie's outburst was accompanied by more sobs and sniffles along with the steady creaking sound.

Tanna closed her eyes as tears flowed down her cheeks. "Tell me where you are, Vonnie. I can help you if you just tell me."

"Don't ask for me tomorrow. And don't worry. There won't be any kids here. I wouldn't do that to them."

The creaking stopped and Tanna yelled into the phone, "Vonnie! Where are you?" No sound came from her phone.

With shaking hands, Tanna pushed redial, but it went straight to voicemail. "Lord, tell me where she is, *please.*"

Tanna started the car, ready to frantically drive up and down the streets, but she knew that would be useless. That rhythmic creaking sound...where had she heard that before, and why wouldn't there be kids there tomorrow? Where? She scrunched up her face and held her head in her hands. Why did the phrase, "ask for me tomorrow," sound so familiar?

Like a flash, Tanna knew the words were from *Romeo and Juliet*. Mercutio said them when he was dying. Suddenly, she snapped her head up and jammed the car into drive.

The swings on the playground made that creaking noise.

Tanna saw a figure standing on one of the swings as she drove up to the curb. Leaving her door open, Tanna ran to the swings, calling Vonnie's name. She wrapped her arms around the swing encircling and lifting Vonnie. "Jesus, help me!"

Both of them collapsed in a heap on the snow-covered playground. A rope was wrapped around Vonnie's neck, but the end was not attached to anything. "I couldn't do it." Vonnie gulped between sobs as Tanna sat up and removed the rope from her neck.

Cradling the teen like a small child, Tanna rocked her until her tears were replaced with violent shivers. "Let's get you to your house where it's warm."

"No, I can't go there." Vonnie pulled away, and Tanna was worried she would run.

"Why can't you go there? Aren't your grandparents home?"

"I don't know, but those guys are probably still there, and I don't like the way they look at me."

Tanna's brows drew together as she looked into Vonnie's fearful eyes. "Your cousin?"

"No, his friends. My grandma won't let them in the house if she's home, but they just kind of barged in when they found out my cousin and I were there alone."

Tanna hesitantly asked, "Did they do anything to you?"

"Not really, but I didn't want to be around them when they started drinking." Tears flooded her eyes as she continued. "I just wanted my Dad to be there to protect me, but he doesn't care what happens to me anymore."

Tanna gingerly rose to her feet and extended her hand to help Vonnie up. With her arm clasped firmly around Vonnie's waist, Tanna steered her to the car. They sat in silence for a few minutes while Tanna bit her lip, trying to decide what to do next. Finally, she drove to Sarah's house.

"My mom lives here. Let's go in." Tanna gently touched Vonnie's arm. "You'll be safe here."

"Is Tucker here?" Vonnie looked sideways at Tanna.

"Yes, but hopefully he's sleeping. Why?"

Vonnie pushed herself back against the seat. "You won't tell him what I did, will you?"

"No. Vonnie, I promise I won't tell Tucker anything about what happened on the playground. Now, let's go inside where it's warm."

Sarah sat at the table with her Bible open when Tanna and Vonnie walked in the door. She stood and hesitantly approached them. Gratitude and caution filled her eyes as she looked from Vonnie to Tanna.

"Mom, this is Vonnie, and we're cold. How about some hot cocoa?"

"Nice to meet you, Vonnie. Sit here." Sarah motioned for Vonnie to sit in a chair at the table, and she set a sauce pan on the stove to heat the milk. Tanna wearily stood behind Vonnie and looked at Sarah with an expression that said she had more questions than answers for the young girl with her.

"I'm going to change out of these clothes. I'll be right back." Tanna walked around Vonnie to face her.

"Sure. Whatever." Vonnie shrugged and lowered her eyes.

Sarah smiled assuredly. "We'll be just fine. The milk is almost warm. I just have to add the chocolate."

As she stirred the chocolate into the warm milk, Sarah looked over her shoulder and saw Vonnie looking at the page in her open Bible on the table. Before reaching for the mugs on the counter, she paused and closed her eyes for a moment to whisper a prayer.

"Excuse me, miss… Sorry, I don't know your last name."

Sarah barely heard Vonnie's faltering statement, but she understood enough to turn and smile. "Just call me Sarah. That's fine with me."

"Uh, Sarah, what does this mean?" Vonnie pointed to a verse in the Bible.

Sarah set the three mugs on the table. "Could you read it to me while I pour the cocoa?"

The panicked expression on Vonnie's face caused Sarah to turn so the girl wouldn't see the hopeful smile on her face. *Thank you, Lord. I couldn't have planned it better. Give me the words you want her to hear.*

"'Those who know the Lord trust him, because he will not leave those who come to him.'" Vonnie looked up.

"What do you think it means?" Sarah held Vonnie's gaze until she dropped it to take a sip of cocoa.

Vonnie shook her head and lowered her eyes to the open Bible.

"Here, drink your cocoa." Sarah slid a mug closer to Vonnie. "I'll do what I can to explain what that verse means."

Vonnie sipped her cocoa with her luminous, dark, brown eyes peeking over the edge of the cup.

"I'm not going to give you the whole background of this verse, but it was written by David, who knew that he could trust God not to ever leave him alone."

Vonnie tilted her head. "How could he know that for sure? Was he, like, really perfect?"

"Oh, no. David wasn't perfect, but God loved him anyway. You don't have to be perfect for God to love you. He just does, and because He loves you, He won't ever leave you all alone."

"You mean..." Vonnie pressed her lips together when Tanna walked in the room.

"I didn't mean to interrupt. Here are some clothes for you if you'd like to change, Vonnie."

Vonnie eyed the clothes Tanna held out to her and mumbled, "Could I take a shower?"

"I think that would be alright. Don't you, Mom?"

Sarah hesitated but stood. "Follow me. I'll show you where everything is."

After Sarah returned to the kitchen, Tanna positioned herself at the table so she could see the bathroom door before she told her mom in hushed tones the events of the night. Sarah gasped and she bit her lower lip as Tanna described Vonnie standing on the swing with the rope around her neck.

Sarah anxiously glanced down the hall. "Should we check on her in the bathroom?"

"I don't think she wanted to go through with it, so I think she'll be fine for now. I called the dean of students, and she said to keep her here while she contacts her aunt and social services. She said if Vonnie trusted me enough to stop her, this is the best place for her right now. Do you care if she sleeps in my bedroom?"

"Let's put her in my bedroom. It's quieter, and Tucker won't run in there looking for you."

"Are you sure, Mom? You look like you could use a little sleep."

"I often sleep in the recliner, so don't worry about me. Just take care of yourself and that sweet girl."

―――

Tanna walked to her room but stopped on the way to peek in on Tucker, who was sprawled sideways across his bed, lying face up and looking completely vulnerable.

Lord, show us how to create a secure home for our children where they will never have to doubt our love for them.

Too wound up to sleep, Tanna turned on her cell phone but quickly lost interest in reading social media posts. She really wanted to talk to Josh, but she knew if she called him there would be a flood of tears. He would offer to come, and she would feel guilty for disturbing his rest and possibly waking Jaz. She finally decided if she texted him, he might see it and call her.

Hey,

If you see this before morning, please call me. (Tucker, Mom, and I are fine. Don't worry.)

Tanna set her phone on the table beside her bed and stared at it. Was there anyone she could call? She scrolled through her contacts and caught a glimpse of the time. It was too late to call anyone, and she restlessly walked around the bed to the window. It seemed like hours since she had returned with Vonnie. The whole incident seemed like a bad dream, but the bruises on her arm and hip from falling with Vonnie were a reminder that it was real. She jumped and grabbed her phone when she heard the Mozart sonata.

"Hello."

"Hey. It's me. What's up?"

"I'm sorry. I..." Tanna couldn't squeak out another coherent word.

"Don't be sorry, Babe. Just relax and take a deep breath. When you're ready, I'll be here."

Tanna softly wept while her husband assured her everything would be okay. His soft, loving words continued until her tears subsided. Tanna managed to tell him in bits and pieces about Vonnie and her night. When she paused, he told her he could be on his way to town in a few minutes if that's what she wanted.

"No. It's enough that I heard your voice. I needed that. I don't know what I'd do without you."

"I'm not goin' anywhere."

They continued to talk until Tanna said they both needed some rest. "I think Tucker is fine, so we'll drive to the ranch tomorrow. We can talk while the kids are snowmobiling with Pete."

"I'm looking forward to it. We have a lot to talk about, but would you do something for me?"

"Sure. I owe you after tonight."

"I think you'll like this. Read Psalm 73:26. We'll talk about it tomorrow, but it's important for both of us to know and understand this verse." Josh waited for Tanna to respond.

"Is this an assignment?" Tanna giggled.

"That sounds more like my Little T. I love you, ya know."

"I love you, too, Josh."

CHAPTER TWENTY

Sarah woke from an apparently dreamless sleep to see sunlight streaming in the window and Tucker standing beside her recliner, watching her. "Good morning, Tucker. You're up early. How do you feel?"

"Good. Why are you sleeping out here?"

"I woke up in the middle of the night, so I just decided to sleep here." Sarah hoped Tucker wouldn't ask more questions. So far, she had been truthful with him.

"Where's Mommy?"

"She's sleeping. Let's go in the kitchen and make something for breakfast. Are you hungry?"

"Uh huh. I'll go wake up Mommy."

"No, wait!" Sarah grabbed Tucker before he could dash to Tanna's room. "How would you like to go to the cafe and have chocolate chip pancakes?"

"Can they make dinosaur pancakes?" Tucker lifted an eyebrow.

"I think that's a possibility. Let's get dressed."

"I'll wake Mommy up cause she'll want dinosaur chocolate chip pancakes, too. Do they have coffee?"

"I'm sure they have coffee. But how about we let Mommy sleep? We could order some food for her and bring it back."

Tucker scrunched up his face, closing one eye and peeking at Sarah with the other eye. "What will she think if she wakes up and we're gone?"

Sarah put her hand on her grandson's arm. "I'll leave her a note and maybe call her before we order for her. Okay?"

Tucker thought for a moment. "Let's go because Mommy is normally hungry on Saturday morning. She won't want to wait."

After Sarah made sure Tucker changed into clean clothes, she wrote a note to Tanna telling her where they were going and to call when they were ready for Tucker to come home. After what Tanna told her last night, she didn't think Vonnie would want to explain to Tucker her reason for being there. She slipped into Tanna's room to wake her without letting Tucker know what she was doing.

Tucker had just devoured the head of his dinosaur when Sarah's phone rang. Tanna explained that Vonnie's aunt and a social worker were on their way. "I think if you can delay coming home for about thirty minutes, we should be in the clear."

"How is everyone this morning?" Sarah looked at Tucker, hoping he hadn't noticed the 'everyone' reference, but he was busy talking to his dinosaur.

"We're tired, but Vonnie is calm and accepts the idea that she needs counseling. She made me promise to ask if you would pray for her. She went back to your room after we ate breakfast, and she took your Bible with her."

"Oh, thank You, Jesus. Tell her she can keep my Bible."

"Mom, I think someone is at the door. See you later. Pray for us. This won't be easy."

Sarah inwardly cringed when she noticed Tucker's inquisitive expression. She clicked off her phone under

My Portion Forever

Tucker's watchful gaze. "Was that Mommy? Did you ask her what she wants us to order for her?"

"She ate breakfast, so we don't have to order anything for her, but we could bring her a surprise. What do you think she would like?" Sarah prayed Tucker would forget the rest of her conversation with Tanna.

"I dunno. She doesn't like to eat things that make her into a cubby. Would a donut do that?"

Sarah couldn't help smiling about her grandson's vocabulary. He had an amazing ability to recall expressions he'd heard, but occasionally, he got it wrong. "How about if you pick out what you like, and if she doesn't want it, you can have it."

Tucker's excited expression fell. "Um, I have to ask Mommy before I can have treats. I guess she doesn't want me to be a cubby either, but I don't actually know what that means because sometimes she calls me her cute little cubby."

Sarah thought she knew the word Tucker was trying to imitate, but she needed to prolong their conversation. They still had fifteen minutes before they could go home. "Let's see if we can figure it out. What is Mommy talking about when she says she doesn't want to be cubby?"

"She doesn't want to look like this." Tucker filled his cheeks with air.

"That's what I thought, but, Tucker, the word is 'chubby.'" Sarah emphasized the *ch* sound at the beginning of the word. "Say it like this: *chubby*."

Tucker said, "chubby," and beamed proudly when Sarah lightly clapped for him. "Let's get the donut with chocolate frosting and sprinkles so we can go to your house."

Sarah looked at her watch and wondered how to delay

leaving, but Josh came to the rescue with a well-timed phone call.

"Josh, is anything wrong?"

"No. I just know that Tanna likes to sleep late on Saturday mornings, so I didn't want to disturb her. How is Tucker?"

"If his appetite is any indication, he's back to normal. Maybe better. Here, you can ask him yourself, and then I want to talk to you again."

After Tucker finished talking to his dad, Sarah decided she had delayed long enough. Tucker handed her the phone, and she asked Josh to hold just a minute. Then, Tucker's eyes grew large when she asked the waitress to help Tucker choose five donuts to go.

"Josh, I think your wife would appreciate a visit from you this morning. I'll let her tell you the details, but I think she needs you after last night."

"I was actually hoping to do just that. Let's surprise her, though."

"I won't tell her you're coming. Here comes Tucker, so I'll see you later." Sarah clicked off her phone as Tucker proudly walked to the table followed closely by the waitress, carrying a box of donuts. Sarah paid the bill and drove Tucker to her house, taking a slight detour just in case Vonnie hadn't left yet. She whispered a prayer for Vonnie as she drove.

Tanna threw open the door into the garage before the car came to a stop. She helped Tucker unbuckle his seatbelt and hugged him tightly. "Mommy, I can't breathe," he giggled. "We brought donuts for you. I picked them out."

Sarah thought Tanna looked weary and somehow older, but she was trying her best to be cheerful for Tucker.

"Let's go have some donuts! Is there any coffee, or should I make some?"

My Portion Forever

"I didn't have coffee this morning. That sounds great, Mom." Tanna wandered to the couch and sat down. Tucker crawled into her lap and wrapped his arms around her neck. If Tucker noticed her glossy eyes, he didn't say anything.

Sarah had just placed cups and napkins on the table when the doorbell rang. Tucker jumped off Tanna's lap but looked back for permission before opening the door. She nodded her approval and stood.

"Daddy!" Tucker flung himself at Josh, and Jaz crowded around them to find Sarah. "Do we get to go snowmobiling today?"

Sarah crouched to be eye level with Jaz. "I just talked to Millie, and they are ready for us whenever we want to go, but how about a donut first?"

"Yay! Jaz you gotta see these. They look so delicious, and they have sprinkles!" Tucker pulled his sister to the table.

"Pack your suitcases before you have donuts because after you go snowmobiling with Pete, I think it's time for my family to move back home." Josh tentatively looked at his wife. "I want my family back." He opened his arms, and Tanna stepped into his embrace

Sarah watched Tanna draw back and stare in awe at her husband. "You're the one. You've always been the one."

EPILOGUE

To my dear husband on our anniversary,

Eleven years ago, I walked down the aisle to marry you, a man who has held my heart for most of my life. You are a patient and gentle man who shares my joys and burdens as if they were your own. I love you.

When my brother Matt brought you home all those years ago, I lost my heart to you. It all started as an adolescent crush, but even when you were treating me like a little sister, you listened to me—really listened. Your big brown eyes seemed to look deeply into my heart and grab a hold of it. I was a goner, but then you told me it wouldn't work.

I tried to forget you, but then a misplaced letter changed everything.

We know what happened next, and here we are. My crush turned into a deep abiding love, and I began to really think of you as my Boaz, my redeemer. You were everything to me, and I really didn't think I could survive without you. In short, you became my God. The problem was that only God is perfect, so you couldn't live up to my expectations, and I became disappointed. I thought I had made a terrible mistake.

It took that fateful winter night on a playground with a troubled teenager to make me realize that you are the only husband I want when the road is rocky and the hills are steep. I can't imagine having anyone but you by my side on this journey. You are everything I ever desired in a husband. Thank you for helping me understand that I expected more from you than you could give me. You tried. I know that now. I see it every day, but there are just things in life that only God can provide. You love me but not with the perfect love God has for me.

I realized after our long talk the next day that up to that point, I wanted Jesus to save me from my sins, but I hadn't allowed Him to be the Lord of my life. That's a position I gave you. There's nothing you wouldn't do for me if you could, but that's not always possible. When God created man and woman, He never intended either of them to take His place with the other.

When I was growing up, I thought my parents had a perfect union, but I didn't realize that when my wonderful dad tried so hard to be everything to Mom, he deprived her of the blessings only God provides.

The romantic and idealistic ideas I had about love and

marriage began to change after that. Together with you and Mom, we searched the scriptures and discovered that many of our expectations for our mates were not possible. I'm writing them down here so I never again expect from you what only God can give me. At least, I'm going to try to follow that. (I guess the teacher in me is saying, "If you write it down, you'll remember it." By the way, ignore all grammatical errors; I'm speaking—okay, writing—from the heart, and my heart doesn't always follow rules.)

Before I tell you what I no longer expect from you, I want to tell you what I love and appreciate about you.

- *You care about what is important to me. You tolerate my quirky friend, Monica, because you know I want her to see how a good man treats a woman. (I think she gets it now.)*
- *The hours we prayed together for Vonnie's family have put her on the path to a better relationship with her parents and have created a bond between us that I'll always cherish. (We make a good team.)*
- *You are the "bestest Dad ever." (I heard that from a couple of very reliable sources.)*
- *You treated my mom like your own mom when you dropped everything to take her to Minneapolis for a surgical procedure to alleviate her extreme pain after she was diagnosed with trigeminal neuralgia. (I know she loves and appreciates you, too.)*
- *Finally, I will always be thankful that you listened to God and saved me from marrying the wrong man. (I know I can trust you with our future and family.)*

Now, I'll list the things I pledge not to expect from you, and I ask you not to expect them from me, either.

- *I accept that your way of expressing love will not always satisfy me. God is love, and there's never a doubt that He does everything out of love. (Let's never stop trying to learn which language of the heart speaks to each of us.)*
- *I admit that we have both changed in some ways. We are not immutable, but God is. We can depend on that. (I hope we never quit growing and changing together.)*
- *I pledge to remember that neither of us is righteous. Only God is always right. (I'll agree right here and now that you recall dates better than I do.)*
- *I will not expect you to know everything and be present everywhere. Only God is omniscient and omnipotent. He knows everything about me, including my fears and insecurities. My unspoken desires, thoughts, and sorrows do not escape His attention, and He collects my tears. I will make it very clear when I want you to know something I'm thinking or wanting, but I'll keep in mind that you are not omnipotent. (I would appreciate you fixing the leaky faucet, though.)*
- *I understand that you're not as forgiving of my weaknesses as God, but let's keep trying to be merciful. (I'm really sorry I turned your underwear pink when I accidentally washed them with my red sweatshirt.)*

By the way, I wrote all of this in a letter because that's how this journey started for us. After I finally received that misplaced letter and contacted you, you told me I had to make a choice before we could go any further. Either I wanted to marry Josh Swenson, as planned, or pursue a relationship with you. You didn't make any promises then, but you did tell me you doubted you could be a husband like my dad, so if that was the criterion, it would never work for us.

When I asked why you had initially hesitated to have a relationship with me, you said you were afraid you weren't good enough, but God told you to let me make that decision. After you told me I should only marry someone I was absolutely positive God had chosen for me, I imagined who I wanted to grow old with, and you were the only one who consistently came to mind.

Telling Josh Swenson that I couldn't marry him was one of the hardest things I've ever done. When I called off the wedding, he told me he had always known that he didn't have my whole heart. If I had known then what I know now, I would never have made the mistake of offering it all to him. My heart belongs to God, but I know there is also more than enough room for the husband God chose for me.

I won't risk this letter ending up wedged between the counters at the post office because I plan to deliver it personally to you, my forever husband.

Did God write our love story, or did He make it right? Either way, I know now that nothing on earth replaces God. He is my portion forever.

Your forever wife,
Tanna

QUESTIONS FOR DISCUSSION

1. At the beginning, which Josh did you think Tanna would choose? Why? Did your opinion change as you read the novel?

2. What did you or your spouse look for when seeking a husband or wife? Were your expectations realistic, and did they change?

3. Have you ever been frustrated because someone couldn't see beyond their perception of you? How did you react? Did Tanna's reaction to Josh Schmidt treating her like a little sister help or hinder their relationship?

4. Sarah advised Tanna to pray and wait. Why do you think Tanna rushed to marry Josh Swenson?

5. Have you ever started a new school or job where you knew no one? How did you handle it?

Questions for Discussion

6. How was your behavior as a student in school? Do you agree that most students who are discipline problems in school have an underlying problem?

7. How would you have answered the student's question about marriage? Have you ever thought of marriage as having someone who would never leave you? Is that a good description of marriage?

8. What caused Tanna to doubt she had chosen the right man? At that point, who did you think she had chosen? Why?

9. Why did Tanna think her parents had a perfect marriage? Is a perfect marriage possible?

10. Does an age difference in a marriage matter? How much is too much?

11. Did you ever tell a family secret when you were a child? Should children be taught to keep family conversations private?

12. Have you ever known someone like Monica? What is her purpose in the story?

13. Why did Tucker and Vonnie seem to hit it off when Vonnie couldn't get along with anyone else?

14. There is evidence that Tanna loves her husband, so why is she unhappy with him? Is it possible to love someone and be disappointed at the same time?

Questions for Discussion

15. Why was it so easy for Sarah to let Sam do everything for her? How did that impact her marriage and family?

16. Josh hid a secret from Tanna about her parents. Should a spouse keep something from his mate for any reason?

17. How did the trauma with Vonnie reveal to Tanna that she was with the right man?

18. When did you know which man Tanna chose to marry?

19. What are things that we expect from others that only God can give? Why do we expect our spouses to try to fulfill those desires?

20. Do your spouse's demonstrations of love always satisfy you? Is there anything you can or should do to change that?

21. Can we ever give our whole heart to someone when it belongs to God?

22. How is God your portion forever?

ACKNOWLEDGMENTS

My family and friends listened to endless tales about "my book" for years, and I am deeply grateful for all your prayers and encouraging words.

The members of *Georgia Schmeichel's Book Group* have been an endless source of advice, encouragement, and prayers whenever I needed them. You will never know how helpful you have been. Karen Rickerl Muellerleile, Courtney Stiegelmeier, Amanda Schmeichel, and Deb Stotz were meticulous proofreaders. Any missed errors are my fault.

Sarah Hanks generously gave of her time to offer helpful editing suggestions. Tanna Huber made my photo session an enjoyable morning, and Heidi Shearer captivatingly wrote my author bio. Thank you for sharing your talents.

ABOUT THE AUTHOR

Georgia Schmeichel is a wife, Mom, Grammy/Mimi, author, former teacher, mender of jeans, voracious reader, and Jesus follower. She grew up in a Christian family where she regularly attended church but didn't accept the saving grace of Jesus until one summer at Bible camp when she was fifteen years old. Two years later, she found her calling to be a high school English teacher, but her passion was to follow Jesus' example and write stories with a message. A self-described procrastinator and non-multitasker, Georgia waited thirty-three years until she retired from teaching to write a novel. Rural South Dakota is her home where she and her husband Dale live within driving and walking distance of their son's and two daughters' families. They appreciate living in the wide-open spaces where they can enjoy visits from their eleven extremely active and delightful grandchildren.